"I don't want to scare you, but I need you to know my intentions. I'd like us to see where our relationship can go."

She looked into his eyes, her pulse charging through her, her heart in her throat. This was a time for honesty, if she could only find it. "I understand your feelings. My heart turns to mush when I watch you with Joey. You're loving and caring. You'd make a good father, and I never doubted you would be a wonderful husband. Never."

"Then what is it, Ashley? What causes you to back away sometimes?"

"It's not you. The problem is what you do. Firefighting." She'd said it. Finally. She'd admitted aloud the deep horrible terror that she faced daily since she admitted her feelings for him. "It's the fear, Devon. That's it. Nothing more, and it's something you can't fix or change. I would never think of asking you to leave a career that means the world to you. It would destroy the generous, loving person that you are. I will not be responsible."

Books by Gail Gaymer Martin

Love Inspired

*Loving Treasures
*Loving Hearts
 Easter Blessings
  "The Butterfly Garden"
 The Harvest
  "All Good Gifts"
*Loving Ways
*Loving Care
 Adam's Promise
*Loving Promises
*Loving Feelings
*Loving Tenderness
†In His Eyes
†With Christmas in His Heart
†In His Dreams
†Family in His Heart
 Dad in Training
 Groom in Training

 Bride in Training
**A Dad of His Own
**A Family of Their Own
 Christmas Gifts
  "Small Town Christmas"
**A Dream of His Own
 Her Valentine Hero
 The Firefighter's New Family

Steeple Hill Books

The Christmas Kite
Finding Christmas
That Christmas Feeling
 "Christmas Moon"

*Loving
†Michigan Islands
**Dreams Come True

GAIL GAYMER MARTIN

is an award-winning author, writing women's fiction, romance and romance suspense with over three million books in print. Gail is the author of twenty-eight worship resource books and *Writing the Christian Romance* released by Writer's Digest Books. She is a cofounder of American Christian Fiction Writers, a member of the ACFW Great Lakes Chapter, member of RWA and three RWA chapters.

A former counselor and educator, Gail has enjoyed this career since her first book in 1998. This book is her fiftieth novel. When not writing, she enjoys traveling, speaking at churches and libraries and presenting writing workshops across the country. Music is another love, and she spends many hours involved in singing as a soloist, praise leader and choir member at her church, where she also plays handbells and hand chimes. She sings with one of the finest Christian chorales in Michigan, the Detroit Lutheran Singers. A lifelong resident of Michigan, she lives with her husband, Bob, in the Detroit suburbs. Visit her website at www.gailmartin.com, write to her at P.O. Box 760063, Lathrup Village, MI 48076, or at authorgailmartin@aol.com.

The Firefighter's New Family

Gail Gaymer Martin

HARLEQUIN® LOVE INSPIRED®

Recycling programs
for this product may
not exist in your area.

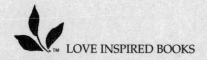 LOVE INSPIRED BOOKS

ISBN-13: 978-0-373-04273-9

THE FIREFIGHTER'S NEW FAMILY

www.Harlequin.com

Printed in U.S.A.

When you pass through the waters, I will be with you; and when you pass through the rivers, they will not sweep over you. When you walk through the fire, you will not be burned.

—Isaiah 43:2

Many thanks to the firefighters Tim Kohlbeck and Chuck Harris, who provided me with a multitude of accurate information on the lives and work of firefighters. Thanks also to Gino Salciccoli, MD, for his assistance in the medical area of this story. As always, I send my love and thanks to my husband, Bob, for his support, love, patience and appreciation for my career. He's also a good proofreader, and he works free of charge... plus he has a great sense of humor.

Chapter One

Devon Murphy pulled into his driveway and closed his eyes, mentally and physically drained. His back throbbed, muscles ached and lungs burned from exertion after he and his fellow firefighters had spent all night responding to the storm emergencies. His body cried for rest.

His eyes stung as he opened them. Though the sky was still weighted with ominous clouds, he hoped the worst was over. Tornado season ripped through towns without mercy. Lovely homes sat along the streets now with damaged roofs hidden behind huge trees pulled out by the roots as if they were weeds in a garden.

Grateful that his neighborhood had escaped the spring storm, he longed for a shower and sleep, but rest came hard when rolling images relived the destructive night following the wind's devastation on nearby neighborhoods.

He grasped the SUV's door handle, flinching as a trash can shot like a missile past his windshield. Stunned by the power of the new wind shear, he sucked in air, watching an anonymous lawn chair tumble through his front yard and tangle in a shrub. Limbs from his neighbor's maple toppled to the ground as if they were pickup sticks.

A few houses away, sparks alerted him electrical wires were down, and he pulled out his cell phone, hit 911 and waited to hear the dispatcher's voice. "Ann, this is Lieutenant Murphy of the Ferndale Fire Department. Another microburst just hit the West Drayton area. Electrical wires and trees are down. Send out Detroit Energy and Consumers Energy to check downed lines and possible gas leaks."

When he heard her say, "Help's on the way," he ended the call and surveyed the damage. As he headed toward the downed lines, a child's cry jerked his attention across the street. The toddler stood beside an up-rooted tree, one limb jutting through the front-room picture window while the rest covered the driveway and part of the lawn.

Devon darted across the street, dodging a fallen tree limb and scooped the toddler into his arms. "Why are you out here alone, son? Where's your mother?"

The boy's tears rolled down his cheeks as he clutched Devon's neck. "Mama's under the tree." With hiccuping sobs and fear growing in his eyes, the toddler pointed at the tree.

Devon dashed around the trunk, stepping over broken limbs while clutching the boy to his chest. His gaze swept over the limbs sprouting new leaves and blocking his view. His own fear heightened. Where was she?

"Mama, get up." The toddler flailed his arms toward a heavy limb close to the side door.

He scanned the area and noticed a red wagon among the limbs. As he moved closer, encouraged by the boy's thrashing arms, he spotted the woman, her dark brown hair splayed across the concrete, her left leg pinned beneath a heavy branch.

After he made his way through the fallen debris, careful not to jar her, he leaned closer, praying she was alive. He hugged the toddler closer and found the woman's wrist, feeling for a pulse. Relief flooded him as he felt the faint but steady beat. Below the tree limb, a trail of blood spotted her pant leg.

Her name? He'd seen the boy and his mother before in the yard, but he'd never had a conversation with her other than a pleasant greeting or a nod. "Ma'am. Can you hear me?"

"Not ma'am. She's Mama."

His eyes shifted to the toddler's anxious face while the boy peered at him and accentuated his proclamation. "She's Mama."

Despite his concern, he couldn't stop the smile.

The boy nodded, and from the young one's expression, Devon suspected the child thought he was a bit dense. "What's your name?"

"Joey." He tilted his head as if weighing the question, but his eyes never left his mother.

"How old are you, Joey?"

The boy held up three fingers, his focus unmoving.

"Can you call your mama? Really loud?"

The toddler's vigorous nod accompanied his screeching voice. "Maaa-maaa, wake up."

Hoping the child's voice would trigger results, Devon searched the woman's face.

Her eyelids fluttered.

Relief. "Don't move, ma'am, until—"

"It's Mama." The boy's determination was evident.

He released a breath. "Mama." He needed the toddler out of his arms, but he didn't have the heart to put him down, fearing what he might do. The woman needed to keep still. "Is anyone else in the house, Joey?"

The toddler didn't respond, his eyes focused on his mother.

Devon used his index finger to shift the boy's face toward him. "No one's home? Where's your daddy?"

The boy's expression remained blank.

No daddy? His chest tightened. He'd seen her and the boy outside, sometimes walking and sometimes she pulled him in the wagon. He'd never seen a man, but that didn't mean she didn't have a husband.

The woman's eyes opened, and she tried to lift her head.

"Stay still. Don't move." He placed his hand against her shoulder, encouraging her to remain quiet. "Where do you hurt?"

Fear filled her dazed expression. "What happened?"

"The tree fell, Mama." Joey's voice cut through the air.

"Joey?" Her eyes closed again.

"He's fine. I have him right here." He touched her arm. "What is your name, ma'am?" The salutation flew out before he could stop it.

Her lids flickered, then opened. "Ashley. Ashley Kern."

"Good." He gave her arm a reassuring pat before double-checking the facts. "Are you home alone?"

"It's only me and Joey."

Sirens sounded in the distance, growing nearer every second. "Please try not to move until help comes." He pulled his cell phone from his pocket and hit 911 again. "Ann, this is Lieutenant Murphy. I'm still on West Drayton near Pinehurst. I have a female pinned under a large limb from a fallen tree. She is conscious. Pulse is faint but steady. I see blood on her left pant leg. I suspect she has a bone fracture. Likely a compound fracture with the bleeding. I'll need a paramedic ambulance and HURT."

The child's body stiffened.

"Help's on the way, Lieutenant."

"Mama's hurt?" Fear filled the boy's voice.

He hit End and slipped the phone into his pocket, realizing the child misunderstood. Now he had to appease the boy's fear. "Joey." He bounced the boy on his hip. "HURT is what we call people who know how to lift the tree so we can get your mama out without hurting her." Any more than she was already injured. His stomach churned, viewing the blood and the large limb holding her fast.

As he finished, the first truck pulled across the street. The men dropped to the ground, most heading for the downed wires, but his friend Clint Donatelli dashed across the road toward him, taking in the scene. "What do we have here?"

"This boy's mother's trapped. She's dazed but conscious." He motioned toward her. "I called for help."

Clint crouched beside her and felt her pulse. "You'll be out of here shortly, ma'am." He rose and gave Devon a thumbs-up, then ran to the street and crossed.

A police car pulled up at the curb, and before the officers left the car, new sirens drew closer. "Here they come, Joey. These are the good guys who'll help your mom...mama."

"Good guys." Joey's grip had lessened as confidence replaced his look of fear.

In moments, the ambulance and HURT truck arrived. The men hurried to his side carrying equipment they would need. He stepped back to let them work. While one crew set off air bags beneath the lower and upper part of the limb that anchored Ashley to the concrete, another team built the cribbing, the hardwood structure used to brace the tree's weight if either of the air bags moved and the tree slipped off the bags. Paramedics moved in with a c-collar, splints and a backboard to immobilize her for the ride to the hospital.

Joey's tears flowed again.

He nestled the child closer. "These are the good guys, Joey. See, they're going to lift the big tree away from your mama and then move her to the ambulance so she can go to the hospital to make sure she's okay."

The child's earlier confidence had vanished, even with his reference to the good guys. Devon's stomach knotted while he tried to explain to the toddler what the crew was doing. When Ashley had been strapped to the backboard and shifted from beneath the limb, Devon moved closer, knowing he needed answers about Joey. "Ashley, I need someone to care for your boy. Tell me who to call. I'll explain what happened." He turned to the nearest paramedic. "Are you going to Beaumont Hospital in Royal Oak?"

The medic nodded.

He followed beside Ashley as they carried her down the driveway. "Ashley, is your husband at work?"

Her eyelids lowered. "No husband. Call my sister. Neely Andrews."

Devon pulled out his cell phone. "Joey, your mama will be okay, but she has to go to the hospital so doctors can make everything better.

Fear returned to the toddler's eyes.

Kicking himself, he wished he hadn't mentioned the hospital, but he had to be honest. "Your aunt Neely will come to get you, okay?"

Joey's arms tightened around his neck. "'Kay." Though Joey's voice was hushed, Devon sensed Ashley heard him.

He punched in the numbers as Ashley struggled to relate them. As the phone rang, he shifted away, hoping what Joey heard next didn't upset him. The woman's voice jerked him back to the phone call. "Neely?"

The line was silent a moment. "Yes?"

"This is Lieutenant Murphy from the Ferndale Fire Department." He heard her intake of breath and wished the call could have begun differently. "Your sister Ashley asked me to call."

"Is it a fire? The house? What happened?"

He provided the details as best he could with Joey listening. "Would you like to pick up Joey here, or should I meet you at Beaumont emergency?"

"Beaumont. I'll be there as quickly as I can."

He stopped to relay his destination to Clint and noticed a neighbor standing at a distance. He waved the man over. "Do you know Ashley?"

"Sure. She's a good neighbor, and so's Joey." He chucked the boy under the chin. "Is she okay?"

"She'll be fine."

"Can we keep an eye on Joey for her?" The man opened his arms.

Joey let out a cry. "Mama." He reached toward her. "I want my mama."

"His aunt is meeting us at Beaumont. I think Ashley will feel better knowing he's there, but thanks for the offer." He turned away but stopped. "Can you secure the house?"

"Sure thing. We have a key." He motioned to the broken window. "I'll cover it for her, too. Tell her not to worry."

Before Devon could thank him, a car careened into the man's driveway, and a woman with a halo of white hair jumped out, her hand to her mouth and her eyes wide as a basketball as she darted toward the man. "What happened? Where's Ashley?"

Devon used the distraction to make his exit. House secured. Window covered. Now, Joey. He gave the boy a hug, thinking of his own young daughter and how she might respond in an emergency.

With Kaylee on his mind, he remembered he would need a car seat to transport Joey. He carried him across the street and located the car seat stored in his garage. The plastic he'd used to cover it was dusty, but beneath, the seat looked like new. He grinned, picturing Kaylee strapped in the chair and singing nursery rhymes whenever they went somewhere. Now more than a year older, he'd purchased a larger restraint seat for her.

Once Joey was strapped into the backseat, Devon slid behind the steering wheel and headed toward Beaumont, sending up a prayer for Ashley's well-being.

Searing red burned through Ashley's eyelids. She tried to raise them, but her effort faded in the struggle. Vague memories stirred through her fogged brain. A stormy sky. The wind. Joey's wagon. The tree. That was it. The haze shifted, and she tried again to pry open her eyes.

A cool hand touched her arm. "You're fine. Don't try to move yet."

She'd heard those words before, but it had been a man's voice. A kind voice, like the woman's, but rich and comforting. An image flickered in her mind. Dark windblown hair. Brown tired eyes, but in them, she saw compassion. A bristled jaw. And… And Joey against his chest.

"Joey." She tried to lift her head, but a headache hammered it to the sheet. "Where's Joey?"

"Your son is fine, Mrs. Kern." Ashley felt the woman pat her arm again.

Her chest constricted. "Fine. What does that mean?" She tried to shift her leg to the edge of the mattress, but the weight bound her in place.

"He's in the waiting room with your sister and a nice-looking gentleman."

Waiting room. She turned her head sideways and willed her eyes to focus. This wasn't her bedroom. The railings along her bed. Eggshell-colored walls. Privacy curtains. The blurred memory eased into her mind. The sirens. The tree. The men. The wail of an ambulance. "Where am I? Beaumont Hospital?"

"That's right. Things will be clearer when the anesthetic wears off."

Her pulse tore through her arm. "Anesthetic?" Through the fuzz, she watched the nurse adjust an IV.

"The doctor will be in soon and explain what happened."

Before she could demand answers, the nurse slipped through the curtain. She was alone. Her mind began to clear. Memories one at a time connected. She'd been in the kitchen. Joey had fallen asleep on the sofa as he often did in the late morning, and rather than disturb him, she'd tossed a quilt over him and let him sleep. She'd noticed the May sky, strange clouds that looked threatening. Then she'd remembered her car parked in the driveway with the window down. Why hadn't she pulled it into the garage?

Before she could act, a powerful wind caught Joey's wagon. She'd left it outside the door when they came in from their walk. Another dumb thing she'd done. A lawn chair tumbled through her yard, and fearing the wagon would be caught in the squall, she'd dashed outside and grabbed the wagon handle. That was the last she remembered, except for the vague images that followed when she'd awakened on the ground beneath a heavy limb and Joey was in the man's arms.

Tears edged down her cheeks. She needed to see Joey now. Where was he? Where was the doctor? How long would she have to wait?

Devon tapped his foot, thinking he should leave but not wanting to. Over an hour had passed, and his earlier exhaustion had returned, leaving his brain fried. The day seemed like a dream, but then so many of those days did. Bad dreams. At least this one had a happy ending.

Joey had become his buddy, and when his aunt Neely had arrived, the boy called her name and opened his arms to her. She scooped him up, her questions to him flying fast.

"Who are you?" she'd asked, her question causing him confusion. Then he remembered he wasn't in uniform.

"I'm a neighbor a few houses down from your sister's, but I'm a firefighter. I'd just gotten home from the bad night we've had. Everything here was fine until this storm came out of nowhere. The microburst sent everything sailing."

Joey wiggled free of his aunt's grasp and raised his arms to him, wanting back on his lap, but he hesitated, wondering if it would upset Ashley's sister.

Neely's surprised expression merged with a grin. "You're his hero…which you truly are. If you hadn't found Ash, who knows what would have happened."

"No hero. Just blessed to be there at the right time." He hesitated before asking his nagging question. "Do you know what's happening with Ashley?"

She blinked as if surprised. "I thought you knew. They're setting her leg…with a screw."

"A screw. That means surgery."

She nodded. "They'll let me know when I can see her. She'll be fine. I know my sister." She leaned down and kissed Joey's head. "I am worried about the house, though." A frown flickered on her face. "Anyone could break in with the window—"

His head hurt. "Sorry. I forgot to tell you the gentleman next door said he had a key and he'd take care of blocking the window. Temporary, but it'll secure the house."

"You mean Mr. Wells. Irvin and Peggy. They're thoughtful neighbors." A grin stole to her face. "I feel better knowing they're taking care of it…for now, anyway."

Gratefulness filled her eyes, and he understood the feeling. Being there to help made him grateful. People helping people. It's the way God wanted it to be. Again his thoughts snapped back to the scene. How long would she have lain there without help if he hadn't witnessed the aftermath of the accident?

"Family of Ashley Kern."

He turned toward the doorway. A surgeon stood in the threshold wearing green scrubs.

Neely bounded from the chair. "Will you hang on to Joey?"

Though she asked the question, she didn't wait for his response as she rushed to the doorway and followed the surgeon into the hall.

Devon, letting Joey play with his car keys to keep him distracted, prayed everything went well.

In a minute, Neely returned. He waited, expecting to learn the details. Instead, Neely gave a subtle head nod toward Joey. "I can see her now, but I'm not sure if—" she eyed Joey "—they'll allow him in, so I'll go alone and see if it's possible to take him to see her for a minute." She gave Devon a searching look. "Do you mind staying with Joey?"

First he wanted answers. "I'm happy to, but what's the diagnosis?"

Her gaze shifted to Joey. "Minor concussion and a closed fracture. The bleeding was a surface wound."

Devon nodded. "I was afraid it was a compound fracture."

Her focus shifted to Joey. "I hope they'll let me take him in for a visit. They'd both feel better."

He nodded, admitting to himself he'd feel better, too, if he saw her. "Go ahead. I'll be here."

She managed a half grin. "Thanks." Turning her attention again to the child, she patted his head. "I'll be back in a minute, sweetie. Okay?"

"'Kay." The response was accompanied with the jingle of Devon's keys.

Neely hurried away again, and Joey held up the key ring. "Go for a ride to see Mama."

Devon could barely focus, and he ached everywhere but especially for the boy. "We have to wait, pal. Then maybe you can see her." He prayed they'd let the toddler into the room even for a moment. The child had been brave throughout the whole mess. He was bright as a star and sweet as sugar— maybe like his mom.

Joey rested his head against his shoulder, and Devon closed his eyes a moment. The feel of the boy in his arms took him back to when his daughter Kaylee was about that size. She loved to cuddle, and he loved snuggling to her, smelling the sweetness of her hair and the scent of innocence. As Joey calmed, stillness settled over Devon. He relaxed his shoulders and took advantage of the silence.

"Devon."

He jerked his head and stared bleary eyed at Neely. Joey wriggled against him, arising from his sleep. They'd both gone to dreamland, and now he faced Ashley's sister, embarrassed. "And I'm supposed to be watching this young man."

She shook her head, a calmer look on her face. "Neither of you needed watching. I didn't mean to wake you. I know you've had a horrible night, but they gave me permission to bring Joey down for a few minutes." She bent over and hoisted the toddler in her arms. "You're getting heavy, big boy."

"I'm a big boy." He grinned at her, then turned his dimpled smile to Devon.

Devon pressed his back from the chair cushion and roused himself upward. He realized this ended his excuse for sticking around. "I suppose I should go then."

"Don't go." She raised her hand. "Unless you must. Ashley wants to talk with you a minute if you can wait. I won't be long with him." She touched Joey's cheek. "Or if you're too tired, I can—"

His palm flexed upward to stop her. "No, I'm fine. I'd be happy to stay."

"Thanks. She'll appreciate it." She turned and headed to the door.

He sank into the chair, his heartbeat playing a rhythm against his chest. The sensation threw him. He'd received a thank-you from many people he'd helped during one disaster after another, and he'd never reacted with this kind of anticipation.

He stretched his legs and folded his hands across his empty belly, searching for a logical explanation. The boy. That was it. Joey reminded him of Kaylee. Since she lived with her mother while he had only a few days with her during his off time, he felt cheated. He missed so many firsts and heard about them secondhand.

Divorce was a nightmare, especially when it wasn't his doing. He'd taken months to sort through his emotions and to understand what happened. No affair. No sensible reason. Gina announced she was depressed and unhappy. She needed a change.

A change. The word ripped through him. Everyone needed a change once in a while, but not one that ended a marriage. He'd been a good husband...he thought. A hard worker. A loving husband and father. He asked what he'd done wrong. She said nothing.

Maybe that was it. He'd done nothing. Perhaps her life wasn't exciting enough, while his was too exciting fighting fires and saving lives. He even rescued kittens in trees and dogs trapped in sewer pipes. Sleep swooped over him, and he rubbed his eyes. His head spun with weariness, and he needed to forget the past. She'd wanted a divorce, and his crazy forty-eight-hour shifts complicated having physical custody of Kaylee. Instead, regrettably, he settled for visitation.

He drew in air to clear his mind. Going

over it again solved nothing. It was the way it was, and he'd learned to enjoy the time he had with his sweet daughter.

Devon rose, smelling the acrid coffee coming from the urn. He took a step toward the pot, but his stomach churned. He dismissed the idea. He needed food. No. He needed sleep.

"She's ready to see you."

His pulse skipped hearing Neely's voice.

She shifted Joey in her arms. "I'm going to take this boy home and give him some food and then off to bed. Thanks so much for all you've done. You've been more than kind."

"I'm glad I was there." Somehow the words meant more to him than they should. He gazed at Joey. "And don't worry about the house. I'll check to make sure everything's safe before I hit the sack."

She nodded her thanks and gave him directions to Ashley's room. With another nod, she pivoted, clutching Joey in her arms and heading for the exit.

Devon strode down the hall, his legs pushing him forward, eagerness in his step. Helping a neighbor, anyone, always uplifted him.

But the image of her pinned beneath the trunk depleted his breath. Strange. He'd seen those scenarios many times in his career. People hurt, bleeding, dead. Why this reaction? For one thing, he needed sleep. That had to be all it was.

Chapter Two

Ashley longed to throw her legs over the mattress and head home. She missed Joey even though she knew Neely and her dad would wrap their love around him. She worried about other damages that might have happened to the house besides the broken front window. And then, a shattered window meant someone could break in and steal… Steal what? She didn't have anything worth stealing. Except maybe her computer. That was her most valuable possession.

Well, she could purchase another computer. Photographs, little gifts Adam had given her. Those precious items could never be replaced.

Life was precious. She thanked God her life had been spared. Joey needed her. One parent was better than none. One loving parent was a precious gift to a child. She grinned, recalling while growing up how she had been covered in love by her father.

Footsteps sounded in the hall, a heavier step than the cushioned shoes the nurses wore. Was it him? Neely mentioned his name, but she'd already forgotten. She'd seen him before, mowing his lawn a few houses down the street from hers. She shook her head, recalling that when she'd first opened her foggy eyes, she'd thought he had been an angel. Then she'd focused, noticing the dark bristles on his chin, and calculated angels didn't have to shave. Before the smile faded, her memory became a reality.

He stood in the doorway, looking hesitant.

"Please, come in." She motioned to the only chair in the room. "I'm sure you're tired and want to get out of here." She lifted her shoulders. "I know I do."

A grin brightened his face, but as he moved toward the chair, she spotted more than weariness in his eyes. The expression aroused her curiosity. "At least I'm more alert than I was when you found me." She extended her hand. "Sorry, but I don't remember your name."

He grasped her hand and squeezed. "Devon Murphy. I live on Drayton, too, a few—"

"I know. I've seen you outside sometimes." On her walks, she'd admired the neat two-story home of redbrick with muted moss-green trim. She'd envied the second-floor balcony and sometimes imagined what it might be like to sit there on a summer day. She had also admired his toned build and good looks. "Neely told me you're a firefighter. I couldn't have had a better person than you to find me."

He shrugged. "Most anyone would have done the same. I'm grateful I came home later in the morning than usual because of the storm. When I saw Joey crying alone in the yard, I knew something was wrong."

Her heart gave a kick, envisioning Joey confused and frightened. She shook her head and sent up another prayer of thanksgiving. "I'd left him napping on the sofa…and ran out to save his wagon from being blown down the street and to put my car in the garage. I thought I'd be right back inside." She motioned toward the chair again. "Please."

"Things don't always go as planned." Finally he dropped onto the vinyl cushion and rested his arms on his knees, his fingers woven together. "I stuck around today for Joey. He's my new buddy." He gave her a tired grin. "And to be honest, I wanted to know you were okay."

"I'm fine." She searched his eyes, curious if he visited all the people he'd rescued. "The fuzz is gone from my brain at least. Only a minor concussion, but then anesthetic can turn gray matter to mush, too."

Devon gestured toward her leg beneath the sheet. "And the fracture. I'm sorry about that."

Her leg was another matter. "I'm alive. It could have been worse." She recalled her confusion. "To be honest, I thought you were an angel when I first opened my eyes."

His seriousness fled, and he laughed. "Me. I'd be the one with a tilted halo."

"The Littlest Angel." If he really were an

angel, she would ask for a miracle healing so she could go home.

Devon's grin faded. "How long will you be here?"

"I'm not sure. The surgeon talked in circles, but I hope they let me out tomorrow."

He arched an eyebrow. "That would be a miracle."

Miracle. He'd read her mind.

"You had a surface wound on your thigh and then surgery to set the lower leg with a screw. They'll want to keep an eye on you for a while."

"But..." Tears escaped her eyes and hung on her lashes. She lowered her head, hoping he didn't notice and wanting to be the brave person she'd learned to be when she lost her husband. Before she could wipe the moisture away, tears spilled down her cheeks.

"Ashley?" He sprang up and stood beside the bed, his hand on her arm. "I didn't mean to upset you. I—"

"You were being honest." She raised her head, ignoring the tears. "I'm Joey's only parent, and what will he do without me?"

"I'm really sorry."

His compassion touched her. "Adam died in the Middle East. Afghanistan. He never saw Joey. Never knew his son, and—" The words jammed in her throat. "Sorry. It's been nearly three years, but it still hurts."

"I'm sure it does. I can't imagine." His face filled with tenderness as a distant look in his eyes assured her that he understood her sorrow.

She swallowed, hoping to control her emotions, and she dug deep for strength. "With a toddler, I was blessed to find work I could do at home—secretarial work for a couple of small businesses. And I have a stack of things they need soon. The job's been a life-saver for me. No need to hire someone to care for Joey. Setting my own work schedule." Schedule. Her sister's image flew into her mind. "And Neely. I've really messed up her wedding."

Devon's jaw dropped. "How did you do that?"

She pictured the lovely dress Neely had selected for the attendants. "Her wedding. I'm the matron of honor." She flung her arm toward her leg. "Can you picture me hobbling down the aisle? I'm supposed to be her hands and eyes. But now, my hands will be on crutches and my eyes focused on not falling over."

His concerned expression unraveled and he laughed. "I'm sorry, but you have so many other things to worry about. The wedding doesn't seem like your worst problem. Your sister will love you anyway."

She narrowed her eyes and shot him a glare. "You don't understand."

He drew back, giving her a cockeyed look. "I probably don't."

His expression tickled her, and her irritation slipped away. "I...I shouldn't have taken my self-pity out on you. It's certainly not your fault."

A tender look filled his eyes. "When's the wedding?"

"August. I doubt if I'll be—"

"Think positively. You never know. You could be dancing at the wedding. That's more than two months away."

She shrugged. "I hope. But I can't help think of all the wedding plans I'm supposed to help with…and Joey. Now here I am in the hospital."

"One day at a time." He looked uneasy. "You have Neely's help, and I'm sure—"

"And my dad. He's so good with Joey, but he has things to do." She felt foolish with her uncontrolled emotions as tears rolled down her cheeks. "I just want to go home."

Devon drew a tissue from the box on her tray table and wiped away the moisture. "I know you do, and you will soon enough. Getting around on crutches will be the trick."

"I can do it. If I can lift that boy of mine, I can handle a crutch."

He chuckled again. "He is a heavyweight." He dropped the tissue into the paper receptacle taped to the tray table. "And if either your sister or your dad needs help with Joey, I'll be happy to entertain him for a few hours when I can. I work forty-eights hours on and forty-eight hours off with an occasional Kelly Day thrown in."

"Kelly Day? What's that? An Irish holiday?"

"No holiday or relationship to my Irish surname. Since we aren't paid overtime, we receive extra days off so our workweek meets the Fair Labor laws. A myth says the surname Kelly came from the Chicago mayor who revamped the firefighters' schedule and improved their wages and benefits."

Seeing his grin, she realized he was even more handsome than she remembered. She tried to shift her leg so she could roll to her side, but as always the bandage and ache waylaid her. She appreciated how Devon's playfulness distracted her from her worries even for a little while.

He stood above her, his hand returning to her arm. The warmth rushed to her heart for his kindness. "I'm going to leave and get some shut-eye, and I hope you get well fast and can get home soon."

Ashley pressed her hand against his. "Before you leave, I want to say thank you from the bottom of my heart. You're an A-1 example of a good neighbor. I'll be forever grateful."

"Just get well." He straightened and gave her a wink. "See you soon."

She lifted her hand in a feeble wave, hoping she would see him soon. It sounded nice.

But as his broad shoulders swept through the doorway, the familiar guilt came back. Even when she tried to reason with herself, her late husband, Adam, filled her mind. She felt as if she were cheating on him when she enjoyed another man's company. One day the feeling might pass... Would pass, but for now, she couldn't shake it off.

She feared that having a male friend would crush the new life she'd built for herself and Joey. She'd learned to stand on her own, to be strong and determined. On the other hand, Devon made her smile, and his kindness couldn't be measured. He was an angel in a way, but friendships with the opposite sex, though aimed at being platonic, often led to romance. Months earlier she'd talked herself into a relationship that turned into a disaster. She'd been overconfident he was the real thing. She'd been duped. Even Neely's warning had flown over her head, but her sister had been right. The guy proved to be a lustful drunk, a real snake in the grass.

Enough of him. She blotted him from her thoughts and replaced him with Devon's kind face. He had these mahogany eyes, canopied by straight eyebrows. His lips curved to an amazing smile that made her smile back. If she ever fell in love again, Devon would be the kind of man she would want. He reflected the wonderful attributes she'd loved in Adam.

But Devon had one huge strike against him. She would never align herself with a man whose career put him in danger every day. Adam had been a soldier. Devon, a firefighter. Both careers screamed danger. She wouldn't do that to herself. Not again. Ever.

The red digital numbers pierced his vision and Devon closed his eyelids again. A three-hour nap was all he'd had and even that had been restless. Each time he woke, he relived hearing Joey's cries earlier in the day and finding Ashley under the tree. Too often, the images intruded. He wasn't alone. Every firefighter dealt with the same horrible recollections.

At least he'd done as he promised. When he'd pulled into his driveway from the hospital, he'd checked Ashley's window. As Mr. Wells had promised, he'd patched it with pieces of plywood that had seen better days, but it worked. Still the window required repairing, and the tree needed to be cut and removed. When Ashley came home, he didn't want those problems hanging over her.

He slipped his arm beneath his head and gazed at the ceiling. Even there he could see Ashley beneath the tree. At the hospital when he saw her after the surgery, he'd been blown away by her beautiful eyes, wide-set and as brown as dark chocolate, and arched by brows as sculpted as a bird's wings.

Knowing sleep evaded him, he slipped his legs over the edge of the bed, stretched his arms to the ceiling and dragged air into his aching chest. The short nap would suffice. Dusk hung outside the window. He glanced at the clock. Eight-thirty. Daylight savings time had given him an extra hour of light.

He ambled into the kitchen, filled the coffeemaker and stared into space. Though needing to eat, he wasn't interested in food. Instead, he wondered how Joey was faring and if Ashley had rested after they'd said goodbye earlier. She needed rest since they would have her up soon for physical therapy.

She would learn to use crutches, to walk up the stairs and move around on her own. When she mastered the undertakings and healed to the physician's satisfaction, the reward would be to return home. That was what she wanted, and her drive guaranteed Ashley would do all she could to make it happen. He'd already recognized her staunch character, her determination.

Grateful for the day, he wanted to see what he could do to help with Ashley's house. His own place needed dusting and vacuuming, maybe a load of laundry, but Ashley's home needed more. His own tasks could wait.

The coffee's gurgle roused him. He filled a mug with the pungent brew and pulled out his cell phone before settling at the kitchen table. He searched the call log, spotted Neely's number and hit it. As it rang, he reviewed what he could do to help. After three rings, he raised his finger to end the call. Instead, a man answered. Question sounded in his voice.

"Hi, I'm the firefighter who found Ashley this morning. Is this her sister's number?"

"Devon. That's your name, right?" His

tone became friendly. "Thanks for your help. We're grateful."

He assumed the voice belonged to Neely's fiancé. "No need to thank me. I was at the right place at the right time." He paused. "I didn't catch your name."

"I'm a bit forgetful." He chuckled. "I'm Fred Andrews, Neely's dad. I'm glad you called. You were a hit with Joey."

"He made a hit with me." Devon chuckled. "He's an amazing kid. So smart."

"He is. You can tell I'm a proud grandpa." His voice muffled a moment. "Hang on. Neely wants to say something."

A rustle of noise was broken by Neely's greeting. "I've talked to Ash, and I thought you'd want to know she's doing okay. She slept after we left, and she's a fighter. She'll get out of there as fast as she can. Meanwhile, we'll be with Joey. My dad's available to help, and if he's busy, I can take time off work. Jon, my fiancé, would take a day, too."

His disappointment surprised him. "No other problems then?"

"Well…" She drew out the word. "Now that you ask, the house is another issue, and—"

"That's why I called." His disappointment faded. "I'll be happy to pitch in where I can. I don't have a key, but if you trust me, maybe—"

"Trust you." She sputtered the words with a chuckle. "Goodness, you're more than trustworthy. But I don't want to take advantage—"

"I'm volunteering. I have a couple of days off, so I can help. I know a guy who cuts trees—unless you have someone in mind—and I know another guy who can replace the window. I can give him a call about the situation if you'd like."

"Like? It's perfect, and by the way, I called the insurance company so they know what happened. So, if you're willing…" She covered the mouthpiece a moment and then returned. "How about this? Jon just arrived. He can meet you at the house in ten minutes and give you the key. Will that work?"

"Sure does. I'll watch for his car."

"It's light beige."

"Got it." When he hung up, he rose and dug into the refrigerator. He pulled out bread and slapped salami and pepper jack cheese between the slices. Dinner with no fuss. With a refill on coffee, he walked to the living room window and waited.

His interest in the project boggled him. Dealing with injured people and property damage was a daily event, and he tried to harden himself to it. Otherwise it would eat him raw.

But today he'd experienced a sense of mission, almost as if he had been called to serve in a special way. It had to be the boy. Kids could twist hearts around their tiny fingers. He'd been twisted already when he'd looked at the little boy's face.

His daughter, Kaylee, filled his thoughts again. He should have picked her up today, but her mother had called and asked him to skip the visitation this week. She'd sounded different—slow and calculated. He shouldn't have agreed, but she riled easily. To keep peace, he'd agreed to the change. He'd do anything to avoid arguing. He would see Kaylee on his next days off, but he still didn't like it.

When headlights reflected on the road, he chomped down the final hunk of sandwich.

Though the night darkened by the minute, he could make out a light-colored SUV. He swallowed the last of the coffee, set the mug on the lamp table and stepped outside.

The vehicle pulled in front of Ashley's house, and as Devon neared, Jon slipped from the driver's seat. The man stood tall with broad shoulders and a shock of dark hair.

Devon crossed the street and greeted him in the driveway.

Jon dug into his pocket and dangled a single key from a key ring. "This is kind of you."

"I'm happy to help. I know Ashley is a single mom, and—"

Jon dropped his gaze. "She's been through too much. This kind of thing doesn't help."

Not seeing Kaylee today arose in his thoughts. "It doesn't." But he'd admired Ashley's bravery from the moment they'd met. Questions filled Devon's mind, but he resisted and he hadn't needed to.

Jon released a long sigh. "Adam was a great guy. Kind, loving, faith-filled. He would have been a model dad." Sadness filled his eyes. "He never had a chance. I know that made it more difficult for Ashley. But she only grew stronger. Instead of falling apart, she threw her energy into raising Joey." Pride replaced his sorrow. "The boy's bright like his daddy—not to say Ashley isn't smart—but Adam had something special. I think his son has it, too."

Devon coughed to cover his unexpected emotion and changed the subject. "I'll make those calls I mentioned to Neely, or if you—"

"Yes, thanks. If you'll get estimates, I'll call her insurance company for approval to proceed." Jon extended his hand.

Devon grasped it. "Good plan. I'll give you a call tomorrow."

Jon clasped his shoulder. "Thanks again." Jon shook his hand again and turned down the driveway to his vehicle.

Devon waited until he pulled away, and though temptation to go inside lured him, he didn't. When he was wound up, his body kicked into endurance mode, and the sleep he needed might never come. Tomorrow made more sense. With that settled, he headed home. Maybe if he tried to read or watch a movie, he'd drift off in his recliner. That seemed to happen when he didn't want to sleep. Maybe tonight it would work in his favor.

Devon turned the key in the lock and pushed open the side door. Even though he had permission, walking into someone's house when they weren't home gave him the creeps. He wondered if burglars felt the same way. He took the two steps into the kitchen. A carton of milk sat on the countertop and a loaf of bread stood nearby. Ashley said she'd been in the kitchen when everything happened. He poured out the milk and tossed the carton into a trash can he found beneath the sink. He added "buy milk" to his task list.

He passed through a small dining area into the living room and faced the boarded window. A lamp lay on the floor beside a toppled side table. Across the carpet, glass shards glittered in the daylight from a side window. He righted the table, moving it away from the glass, and surveyed the lamp. No damage. The contents of a candy dish lay scattered nearby. He turned over the dish and replaced the wrapped candies, then set the bowl on the table. A photograph lay face-down. When he lifted it, his heart lurched. A good-looking young man, wearing his Class A uniform, blond hair showing beneath his cap. Adam. He'd been right about Joey's hair color, and now he noticed the similar jaw-line. A father who had never seen his son.

Though he'd learned to control his emotions, pressure pushed behind Devon's eyes. He closed them and set the photo on the table, refusing to weaken. A crying firefighter was useless, but hardening his heart was tough.

He walked into the kitchen, and near the backdoor where he'd seen stairs to the basement, he found a small broom closet. He opened it. No vacuum cleaner. He followed his instincts deeper into the house and located another closet, mainly linens with a small space to squeeze the Hoover. He pushed it into the living room, plugged it in and stepped on the button. The machine's hum filled the silence as he worked it back and forth. When the carpet looked free of glass, he attached an edge tool and inched it along the space close to the wall. Joey played on the floor, he was sure, and he didn't want the boy to get cut.

Standing back, he surveyed the window. Though difficult to measure, he pulled the measure tape from his pocket and did his best to estimate the size in each direction, one large window and two smaller panes. He'd let the expert worry about accurate measurements.

Devon made the two calls before he left the house. Both men promised to call back and come by today as soon as they could, so all he had to do was wait.

After returning the vacuum cleaner to the closet, he passed another row of photographs sitting on a small buffet in the dining room. He walked closer, his stomach tightening. Ashley and Adam's wedding photo wrenched his heart. Two smiling faces beamed into the camera, their arms entwined, a bouquet of white orchids tinged in pink, dark green vines twining between pink rosebuds. A lump formed in his throat, and at that moment, he realized the tears were for himself.

His marriage had ended more strangely than he could ever understand. He and Gina had never argued other than the typical little squabbles all couples had. They'd been in love...he'd thought. When he tried to sort it out, the only clue he found came after her pregnancy. She called it postpartum depression. He'd known of the illness, but had no idea the stress it would add to their lives. Days came when she didn't want to get out of bed. She had lost interest in everything. Her mood swung from anger to withdrawn silence. Even toward Kaylee. Because of his work schedule, she suggested living with her sister who could help her. He watched her go, but he'd tried everything to bring her home. Instead of getting better, she became worse.

The memories tore through him, weighting his chest and curdling his stomach. He loved his daughter. He'd loved Gina, but the love had died. She'd become a woman he no longer knew. He'd failed her. Even prayers and pleading with God had reaped no answer, and finally he stopped, sensing that her choice was God's will. Had he been wrong to think it had been the Lord's decision? He still had no answer to the question.

Thinking of her call, he'd heard a new

desperation in her voice. Something prodded him to call her and demand Kaylee today. He could fight for custody. He turned his eyes to the one window open, which added light to the room. As he looked at the blurred scenery, tears rolled down his cheeks. He brushed them away with the back of his hand, frustrated that he'd allowed himself to succumb to self-pity.

Or was it really pity? Love for his daughter burned in his heart.

He forced himself away from the photographs, not liking the feelings they'd exposed. He scanned the other rooms. Everything looked in order, a few things here and there like any home. Ashley hadn't planned an injury and days in the hospital when she walked out the side door to move her car and salvage Joey's wagon.

Joey. The child would need clothes if he stayed with Neely, and he had the key. He'd call and return it. As the situations organized in his mind, a noise alerted him. He glanced out the front door and saw the window repairman. Once he was gone, he'd leave for the store to pick up milk. Or maybe he'd wait until he learned Ashley's release date.

With Ashley on his mind, he opened the door for the window installer and led him to the living room. While he watched the man work, he reviewed the thoughts skittering through his mind. He wanted to get to know Ashley better. A lady friend sounded nice. A sweet sensation rolled through his chest, but for now, he could only handle friendship.

He had offered his babysitting services to Neely again, thinking about Kaylee and Joey playing together, but the bonus to his plan offered him a chance to bond with Ashley. He liked her. A lot. Though Kaylee was almost a year older, Joey's skills for a three-year-old equaled hers, he was sure. They would get along fine.

But what if they didn't? That could be the end of his plan.

Chapter Three

Ashley closed her eyes, willing away the ache in her arms. She'd hoisted Joey so many times, but lifting her own weight on crutches brought about a whole different challenge. She caught herself more than once forgetting to keep the weight off her left leg.

"One more time."

The therapist's command struck her again, and she wanted to rebel at his insistence even though she knew the therapy was good for her. When she could walk with the crutches, she could go home.

Home. She'd missed her place so much. She'd survived Adam's death. This setback should have been nothing more than a bump in her life. Instead, she'd allowed it to become a dunghill.

Shame swept over her. Strength. Courage. Faith. Those attributes had been her stronghold. Where were they now?

"Ashley. If you want to go home, you—"

"I know. If I want to go home, I have to maneuver stairs. I know. I know." The tone of her voice sickened her.

"Good. So maneuver them."

His cocky comment grated on her patience, but his job consisted of being firm, being supportive and teaching her to walk with crutches. He'd tried firm and supportive. All she'd left for him to use was sarcasm.

She lowered her forehead to her forearm and brushed the perspiration away from her eyes. The stairs took effort and balance. She could do it.

One step at a time, Ashley made her way to the top and back down the other side. "There. How's that?"

"Good. Take a minute and then do it again." His eyes captured hers, and her frustration subsided.

Compassion. The emotion slipped through

her, and she wished she'd not taken her defeated feeling out on him. Without another comment, she moved forward, working her way up and down each step, one at a time.

"Good job." He gave her shoulder a pat. "You're finished for today. In fact, I think you could go home tomorrow."

Her heart skipped a beat. "Really?"

"Your surgeon makes the final decision, but I'll recommend it. I think you're ready."

After four days she was ready. Tomorrow seemed a lifetime, but her gratefulness swelled. "Thank you, and I'm sorry for—"

He put his thick finger to his lips. "Shh. No apologies. I've heard much worse. I've been called names, hit with a crutch—"

"I hope you're kidding."

"Nope. Fact." He rested his hand on her shoulder. "Ashley, be patient with yourself. It won't be easy, and I know you have a toddler at home who you need to care for. Just be careful. No fast moves. Ask for help when you need it, and allow people to be there for you."

He knew her better than she realized. "I'll remember."

She slipped into the wheelchair, and he

gave her an agreeable nod before turning to his next patient. While she waited for an escort to take her to her room, she reviewed what he'd said. Her family had been at her beck and call for so long. They adored Joey, and Adam's death had cut off a slice of their lives, too, but she did find it difficult to ask for help sometimes. Even Devon, her firefighter hero, had stepped into her life, and though she enjoyed talking to him, her discomfort grew, feeling the old guilt as if she shouldn't enjoy another man's company.

"Ready?"

Her head jerked upward, hearing the escort. She managed a smile, and he turned her around and wheeled her back to her room.

Once in bed, she had him prop her pillows so she could sit up and come alive. Her leg ached. Her arms ached. Her head ached. A pill could resolve those issues, but her other problems, ones she didn't understand, couldn't be settled with a pill. She closed her eyes, and Joey filled her mind. He missed her, and she missed him. Terribly. Neely's visit came with stories of his antics. Her father visited and relayed the cute things Joey did when they spent time together. Though she loved hearing their stories, they brought envy. No one should have fun with her son unless she was there to enjoy it.

Foolish, but that was how her mind worked most days.

One other person permeated her quiet moments. Devon. Despite her confusion with guilt and loneliness, she had been unable to control the longing she felt to see him again. Four days had passed with no word from him. Though it made no sense, she felt abandoned. He'd spent the day of her accident waiting in the hospital to make sure she would be okay. He cared for Joey while Neely visited and stuck around to talk with her. That was it.

What did she expect? The answer evaded her. When possibilities slipped into her mind, she chased them away. Getting involved with anyone again—anyone of the opposite sex— would take preparation and contemplation. She'd been duped by her former boyfriend and never wanted that to happen again.

Devon's image drove Erik from her thoughts.

The firefighter had been a concerned neighbor. A gentleman with every meaning of the word. Thinking about a man who had become her hero was senseless, especially a man whose career had "no involvement" written all over it.

She eyed the wall clock. Time for lunch, then one more night in the hospital. Devon's image faded, replaced by her sweet son's face. The image made her grin. Tomorrow. She'd be home.

Devon surveyed the oncoming crew standing around the firehouse apparatus room. "I think that's it. After the last storm, I know we were grateful for the calm evening last night other than Mrs. Benson's falling over her dog again." He grinned. Everyone knew the sweet but lonely lady used every excuse in the book to call firefighters to her home for a few minutes of conversation. The call also meant playing with her dog. She and the mutt loved the attention. "Any questions?"

No one responded except for a couple of murmured comments about dear Mrs. Benson and her dog. He stifled a yawn. "Okay, then. Time for you to work and for us to go home." He grinned, and when he spun around, he rammed into Clint Donatelli. "Sorry, pal. My radar's out of whack." He grinned, too tired to make sense.

"My fault." Clint gave him a pat on the back. "Where you headed in such a hurry?"

"To bed." Devon rubbed his eyes with his knuckle. "But I can only sleep a few hours. I'm picking up Kaylee from preschool this afternoon." He eyed his uniform. "I need to change and be on my way. I thought I'd stop at the hosp—" Why had he said that aloud? He didn't need questions.

A frown shot to Clint's face "Is it your mom? I hope she's not ill."

"No, Mom's fine. It's the... Just a friend." He squirmed at Clint's telling expression, one eye squinting, the other boosting a raised eyebrow.

"Hmm? Could it be a visit with the young woman who was trapped under that tree." Clint's squint segued to a wink.

Devon shrugged. "Okay. Yes. She's a neighbor, and I—"

"If I remember, an attractive neighbor enthralled by the brave firefighter who—"

Devon gave him a poke. "Ever hear of compassion? The woman's stuck in the hospital, missing her three-year-old son who's staying with relatives and probably confused."

Clint wrapped his arm around Devon's shoulders and gave them a shake. "Just razzing you, Dev. You know me, an old man who wished he had someone to go home to."

An unwanted ache slithered through Devon's mind. He'd had similar thoughts more than he wanted to admit. He let Clint's comment slide. "You're not old." Clint was a few years older than his own thirty-three years. "You're seasoned."

"My hair is for sure. Salt and pepper." Clint flashed a grin and ran his fingers through his thick, wavy hair.

Devon gave him a nod. "Salt and pepper looks good on you. But you're right, Clint. I'm afraid the stress is too much for some wives. I have membership in the club no one wants to belong to—divorced men." After the words slipped out, he wished he could take them back.

"Right, and a club where you paid your dues. But at least you had a wife once. She accepted your work enough to marry you."

The comment reminded him of Clint's fiancée walking out on him. "That was a bad situation for you, and I really don't understand why she waited so long to decide she couldn't handle your profession."

"I never understood it either, so I decided no wife is better than being walked out on."

The unintentional blow struck Devon.

"Hey, pal, I'm sorry. I didn't mean that about you." Clint rested his hand on Devon's shoulder. "Anyway, you have a bonus from your marriage. The joy of being a father."

The bonus comment caused Devon to grin. "True." Kaylee had become his greatest joy. "We both have to face the truth. Neither of us is about to change professions. I love my work. Dangerous yes, but fulfilling." He shrugged. "I suppose it's difficult for some people to understand unless they feel the passion we do about saving lives and property."

"It's not you or me, Dev. It takes a special

kind of woman to understand." Clint stared into the distance. "But where are they?"

Devon looked down at his work boots. "You know, sometimes I think about my marriage and wonder what I could have done to make a difference in the outcome. The Lord has a purpose for each of us, and I can't imagine divorce is one of His choices. But it happened." He shrugged. "I keep thinking anyway."

Clint shook his head. "We all question what we did wrong. Maybe I didn't give enough when I was with my fiancée. Maybe..." He lifted his shoulders and released a lengthy breath. "Maybe I'll never know, but I'd like to think I can be a good husband if I had a chance."

Devon nodded. "I'm with you. I hope one day I'll have another chance." He chuckled and laid his palm on Clint's shoulder. "Maybe one day when I'm an old geezer like you."

"Then you think I still have a chance." His grin lightened the conversation.

"I sure do. You'd make any woman a good

husband even if you are a firefighter. Wait and see."

Devon strode to his locker and stepped out of his work gear into his street clothes, but his mind jumped back to the more serious side of their conversation. He'd asked himself many questions after Gina moved in with her sister. "For a while" was how she'd framed it. Worried about her depression and whether she could care for their new daughter, the option seemed the best at the time. But no matter how he sorted it out now, he'd let her down. Now he wondered if love would ever come his way again and if he would ever find someone who could deal with his career.

Clint was right. Only a special woman could grasp how much the job meant to firefighters.

As Devon headed for the exit, his purported plans for the day returned to mind—sleep and stop by the hospital on the way to pick up Kaylee.

He rubbed his forehead, searching for an answer to the question that had just flown into his head. Why visit the hospital? Ashley had enough problems in her life. She wouldn't be that special woman for him, but she was a neighbor, and a special neighbor since he'd come to her rescue a few days earlier.

He could sleep longer if he crossed the hospital off his list. That's what he should do. Why complicate his life?

Since hearing she could go home tomorrow, Ashley couldn't stop her right knee from jiggling, as if the movement would make the time move faster. The clock hands lumbered around the face, seeming as weighted as her left leg, bound in bandages.

Her crutches leaned against the wall. She'd gotten up twice, once to use the bathroom and again to step into the hallway for a short walk with a nurse's assistant. But those short trips disappointed her. She'd hoped that with therapy she would gain strength. Today she felt weaker than usual.

And Joey. She could think of no way to lift him into bed or into his booster seat. How could she do it with crutches and a leg that couldn't bear weight? Her frustration edged on self-pity, and she knew it. Pulling her focus from the wall clock, she studied the crutches. Determination spurred her on, and she slipped from the bed, balancing on her right foot, and leaned toward the crutches. Her left foot hit the floor and pain shot up her leg in a deep throb.

She sank back onto the mattress, tears burning her eyes. Everyone had stressed the importance of staying off the leg until the surgeon deemed it weight bearing. Stupid to get up by herself. Her confidence sank and frustration took its place.

Self-pity. Defeat. Emotions she refused to succumb to. She drew up her shoulders and, using her arms, shifted closer to the wall. This time she dropped to the floor, keeping her left leg safe, and grasped the crutches. "Did it." Her voice surprised her.

Tucking the support under her arms, she tested her weight against the underarm pads and took a step. Determination returned. If she were to manage alone, she needed strength and mobility.

She stepped forward on her right leg and

swung the left, trying to forget the ache in her arms.

"Look what we have here."

Her pulse surged as she looked up. "Devon, I didn't expect to see you."

Like a searchlight, a frown swung across his face. "I hadn't planned to come." His expression read surprise. "But I pass this way to pick up Kaylee from preschool so—"

"She's your daughter."

"Yes. Kaylee's four…almost five, she'll tell you, but that's a long way off." He grinned. "Kindergarten soon. I can't believe it."

The grin faded and sadness registered in his expression, and she sensed he harbored a deep wound. "I've seen her playing in the yard once in a while." But she'd never seen a woman.

He nodded as he eyed his watch. "To be honest, my car just swung into the parking lot."

The image of his car pulling into the parking lot against his will might have caused her to chuckle or roll her eyes, but not today. His unexpected visit surprised her and seemed to surprise him, too.

He fell silent again, and she had so much she wanted to know. She knew better than to push, and judging from his expression, something seemed to be on Devon's mind.

His distant look faded. "Since I'm here…" He grinned. "How are you doing?"

"I'm okay." She'd started to say fine, but that wasn't the truth.

"It's great to see you standing." He stepped deeper into the room. "Any good news?"

"I'm going home tomorrow." Home sounded wonderful, but the pressure of the pads beneath her arm took away the sweetness.

"Home's good. I'm happy for you." A cute grin appeared on his clean-shaven face.

Funny, she kind of missed that rugged look that fitted his strong features. She pulled her gaze away and swung the right crutch upward. "This isn't easy."

"They take getting used to, I hear. And they're not convenient, but the more you practice the better off you'll be." He closed the distance. "Can I help?"

His question confused her a moment until the meaning struck her. "You mean, walk with me?"

He eyed his watch again. "Why not. I have a few minutes, and if anything happens, I'll be there."

Warmth spread through her chest. His offer reminded her of Adam. He'd always wanted to help her, and when she worried about something, he reminded her that if anything happened, he'd be there. Emptiness weighted her chest. Then she looked into Devon's smiling eyes. "Thanks. I'll take you up on your offer."

She made her way to the door while Devon shifted obstacles from her path and stayed as close as he could without tripping over her crutches. The polished hospital floor looked slippery, but the rubber tips of the crutches held fast, and having Devon beside her helped. She never trusted the nurse assistants who ambled beside her. Most weren't any bigger than she was.

She remained silent, making her way down the first hallway, her mind focused on protecting her left leg and the step-swing pattern of her movement. Devon's thoughts were somewhere, too. "Thinking about your daughter?"

He looked surprised at her question. "Always."

Ignoring his reticence, she charged ahead. "I can't even imagine having to share Joey with someone. I'd feel the same even with his father if we were living separately." She couldn't imagine that ever happening between Adam and her. "I've been feeling twinges of envy that Neely and my dad see Joey every day, and I don't." She released a stream of air. "I suppose I could visit with him in the waiting room, but…" She pictured him clinging to her and crying when he had to leave. She couldn't bear it. "I think it would be harder on both of us."

"Tomorrow you'll be home. Everything will be good then."

She hoped. Life would be difficult until she could walk like a normal person. "I hope. I'll need patience until I can dump these crutches."

"Time will fly."

He fell silent. So did she, trying to figure out what happened to change him today. Though he grinned a couple of times, his face looked tense. She expected him to tell her more about Kaylee, maybe Kaylee's mother, but he didn't. She dug for conversation. "Neely said you were helpful getting my house back in order. I can't thank you enough."

"No need. If I'd had a problem like this, I'd like to think someone would be there for me."

Ashley couldn't imagine him without people wanting to help. The man was a giver. "You can count on me, Devon." The offer sailed from her without thinking. How could she provide help? Sometimes she didn't have enough wherewithal to help herself.

"Thanks. One day I may take you up on it." Instead of a grin, he withdrew again.

Her underarms ached with the pressure of her weight, and she questioned how long it would take to get used to it. Silence hung thick again while her mind slid back to his reference to Kaylee. His reticence to talk about his daughter confused her. A caring man had to be a loving father. That seemed logical. She always talked about Joey. She paused, realizing she'd said more to Devon about her life than she did with other strangers.

She wasn't ready to give up yet. "How long will Kaylee be with you?"

His step slowed, almost a pause in movement. She wished she would learn to keep her mouth shut. She could only guess the situation with Kaylee—perhaps her mother—bothered him.

Devon finally looked her way. "Not long enough." His tender tone answered her question.

"I understand. My envy that my family are with Joey while I can't be is ridiculous. But that's what I feel. You must feel the same." She feared she'd overstepped the line of privacy. She needed to back off.

"Your room is close. Ready to go back?"

Her heart sank. Now she'd scared him away. "Yes, and thanks for walking with me. I trusted you would catch me if I stumbled."

He didn't respond. When they reached her doorway, she expected him to say goodbye.

But he didn't. Instead, he followed her into the room and waited as she eased onto the hospital bed. When she'd gotten settled, he set her crutches against the wall beside her and motioned to the chair. "Do you mind?"

"Not at all." The man confused her.

He sank onto the chair and sat a moment, staring at the floor, before he looked at her. "I don't like to talk about myself. Firefighters are supposed to be strong. We save people, so it's not easy to admit—"

"You're not alone, Devon. I don't want to admit where I fail."

"Then you understand, but the difference is you did when you talked about your envy."

"I know, and it surprised me." She worked to get her thoughts in order. No more comments that would upset him. "I don't talk about personal things unless it's with someone I'm close to. Neely, for example." But she'd talked with him. Air drained from her lungs. She gathered her wits. "But you can't shut me up when it comes to Joey."

"Sometimes it hurts."

Ashley longed to know why. Her eyes searched his. "Take a chance. Tell me about Kaylee."

A grin stole to his face. "She's the sweetest little girl in the world. Her mother has had problems that I couldn't help with. I suppose that bothers me more than I admit.

Gina—Kaylee's mother—needed someone available twenty-four hours a day. My job doesn't allow that. She had my thoughts and prayers but not my physical presence. I couldn't—"

"Couldn't, not because you didn't want to. You couldn't be there because you had a community that needed you available and alert. You were in a can't-win situation."

He released a sigh and leaned back against the cushion. "You really do understand."

Adam had been in the same spot. He'd wanted to be with her and Joey, but he'd had a job to do. He'd needed focus and devotion to the military. She understood. Liking it was another thing. She managed a pleasant look and a nod.

"I don't want to talk about Gina, and when I think of Kaylee, her mother comes to mind. I'm still confused." He looked away. "So I don't say much about her, but Kaylee's another story. Maybe you could meet her one day." His face brightened for the first time.

"I'd love to meet her. Our neighborhood doesn't have many children living nearby, so maybe she and Joey could—"

"I thought about that."

She studied his face. "Joey's younger and she might—"

"Joey's bright and verbal. Age doesn't mean a thing in his case. And anyway, she'll love to have someone to play with—" he chuckled "—although a girl would be her preference." He looked heavenward. "Her preference now. When she's older, she'll probably like boys more than I want her to."

Ashley couldn't help but laugh.

Devon stood and smiled. "On that pleasant note, I'd better get to the school or I'll be late." He dug into his pocket and pulled out his car keys. "If I can be of any help, Ashley, let me know. I'm right down the street. I know your first couple of days will be a learning curve for you, but you're a strong woman. I saw that the day I met you. You can do it." He took a step toward her, then faltered and stepped away. "Tomorrow will be here before you know it."

He gave a wave and strode through the door. In the hallway, he paused and waved again.

Before she could respond, he was gone.

An empty feeling swept over her. Concern followed. Devon caused a rush of emotion she hadn't felt in a long time. When Erik appeared in her life, he'd become a novelty, a test run, of being with a man who wasn't Adam. Once again her determination had taken over, and she had wanted to prove to herself and others that she could date and find the man of her dreams. But that dream ended in a nightmare.

Then she faced reality. She needed to think clearly. Why get involved with someone who could never be that special person. Friendship sounded great, but could she monitor the desire to feel complete and whole again. Would she rush a relationship into something else like romance and thoughts of marriage?

Concern rattled her spine. She'd already compared Devon to Adam's wonderful qualities. Comparisons triggered danger, not because of the attributes they shared, but after losing Adam, she wanted a man with a safe job, a business career, anything behind a desk—nine-to-five hours, occasional overtime maybe—but a man who came home from work at night. Not one who lived with danger every moment.

She wanted friendships, someone she could bond with and care about, but without getting romantically involved. Devon's full life didn't leave room for romance, either. Kaylee, his broken marriage, a demanding career. Maybe that could provide a buffer between them.

Her concern lightened. Having someone close who liked Joey and her would be nice. Their kids could play together. Giving it a chance made sense.

But could they remain just friends? The answer shivered down her back. If she perceived the friendship deepening to more than a platonic relationship, she knew what she had to do.

She'd say goodbye.

Chapter Four

Devon gazed out the window toward Ashley's house for the third time that morning. He ran his fingers through his hair with a sigh. He turned away, amazed at his preoccupation with her arrival home from the hospital. He'd done everything he could. He'd purchased the milk, overseen the window repair and called Neely to let her know the cost of the tree removal. Jon had dropped off the money so he could pay the guy. The house was ready.

"Kaylee?" He listened but heard no response. "Are you hungry? Ready for lunch?" His gaze drifted back to the window when he heard a car passing on the street. A red truck. He shook his head. "Kaylee?"

His concern changed from the window to his daughter. He headed down the hall to the staircase and called again. This time he heard a clump. In a moment, Kaylee appeared at the head of the stairs.

"What?"

"That's my question. What are you doing?"

She shrugged.

The shrug was accompanied by a guilty look, and instead of asking, he climbed the stairs and took a few steps from the landing. "Are you hungry?"

She nodded and slipped past him, her foot on the first stair.

Devon reached out and put his arm around her shoulder. "Hold on."

She stood in place without looking at him.

His mind flew from one possibility to the other. "What were you doing?"

"Nothing."

Nothing didn't cause her reaction. "Show me?" His worst thought was playing with matches. She'd never done that, and he only had a couple boxes in the house for lighting candles.

She dragged along beside him, and when

he stepped into the room, he stopped inside the door. His fear washed away, replaced by sadness. A photo album lay open on the floor, an album he knew held memories of happier days. Gina's pregnancy and early pictures of Kaylee. "You're looking at old pictures."

He knew she'd gotten them from a bookshelf in his bedroom, and he ventured her guilt was being in his room without asking. Reprimanding her wasn't his priority. His greatest concern was the awareness that their separated lives today bothered her as much as it did him. She wasn't even five, and he hadn't considered how much the divorce may have affected her.

Devon picked up the album and set it on her bed, then lifted her and placed her beside it. He joined her and opened the cover. "Did you enjoy the pictures?"

She nodded and looked at him for the first time, almost as if she was surprised he hadn't been upset with her. When she looked back at the album, she turned a couple of pages and pointed. "Was that me?"

Her finger rested on the photo of Gina

with her belly protruding beneath a light green blouse.

He chuckled. "It sure was. You arrived about a month later, and let us know you were happy to be in the world."

"I did?" Her gaze shot to his. "Did I talk?"

"Nope. You let out a howl. A happy howl."

Kaylee giggled and turned a few more pages. "And this was me when I was a baby."

Devon lowered his gaze to the row of photographs, close-ups of Kaylee encircled in a pink blanket, Kaylee in his arms and one in her mother's arms. Those days wrapped around him with good memories that had faded into despair as time passed.

Weighted with the recollections, he enfolded Kaylee in his arms and lifted her into his lap. "We can take the pictures downstairs, okay?"

A faint smile curved her lips. "I shouldn't go into your bedroom unless I ask." She tilted her head.

He fought back a grin. "Right." He rose with her in his arms and hoisted her into a safe one-armed position before grabbing the album. "And now, how about lunch?"

"Pizza."

This time he chuckled without restraint. "Not pizza, but something as good. Grilled cheese."

"Yummy." She ran her tongue over her lips, and wrapped her arms around his neck. "I love you, Daddy."

"I love you, too, precious." And she was. He held her close as he traversed the stairs and headed into the kitchen. He lowered her to the floor, and when he did, she hurried to the refrigerator and opened the door. "Can I have milk?"

"Sure can." He set the album on a chair and pulled a glass from the cabinet, filled it with her drink and proceeded to make the sandwiches. He liked them, too.

As they ate, he glanced at the wall clock, his thoughts drifting again to the white house with the new picture window. He'd been upstairs for a while looking at the photographs, and now he wondered.

When he rose to set his dish into the sink, his curiosity got the better of him, and he strolled into the living room and checked across the street. A car sat in the driveway, and his pulse skipped. He turned away, irritated at his irrational emotions, and returned to the kitchen.

Kaylee had ripped off some of the crust and was eating the last of her sandwich. When she finished, she pushed her saucer away before taking a long drink of milk. Before she set down the glass, she grinned at him. "Milk's good with cookies."

He couldn't help but chuckle, happy for the distraction. "One."

A half frown knitted her brow. "Okay."

He reached into the bread box where he'd slipped a package of chocolate chip cookies and handed her one. "When you're done, we can go outside. What do you say?"

She nodded and proceeded to dunk her cookie into the glass. She nearly lost it in the liquid, but she snatched it out and bit. "Good."

He waited while she entertained herself with the cookie-dunking, and when she finished, he rinsed the dishes and put them in the dishwasher, knowing he probably wouldn't see Ashley anyway.

Outside, the afternoon sun warmed his

back as he sat on the porch watching Kaylee search for ladybugs in the flowers. She'd found one once and she seemed to think she'd find more. She never did. Though he kept one eye on her, his glances aimed down the street. Feeling antsy, he rose and refocused. "Let's get your bike and I'll walk alongside you."

Her head jerked up, and the ladybugs took a backseat to the walk idea. They rounded the house and located her bike equipped with training wheels in the garage. She jumped on and pedaled down the driveway, her legs soon too long for its small size. She'd grown up before his eyes.

The same old ache rolled down his back. He didn't want to miss seeing his daughter grow, and even more, he worried about who was raising her. Gina or her sister, Renee. His last conversation with Gina left him feeling edgy. Something in her voice sounded different. He couldn't put his finger on his concern, but it slipped into his subconscious and wouldn't let go. The last thing he wanted to do was grill his daughter, but times rose when he prayed she'd reveal something that would help him understand what bothered him.

Devon hurried to follow Kaylee as she turned on to the sidewalk, and he was glad when she went left, which meant they would be heading toward Ashley's house. As he hurried to catch up to Kaylee, he heard someone call his name. He looked across the street to see Neely waving to him from the driveway. Behind her, Joey appeared from the side of the house.

When the boy saw him, he grinned and toddled toward the street. Neely captured his hand to keep him from venturing into the road.

Devon's heart jigged with the boy's smile. He checked for traffic and then caught Kaylee's attention and beckoned her to follow. He strode beside her as they crossed, and when he hit the sidewalk, Joey opened his arms to him.

"Hey, buddy." Devon hoisted the toddler onto his hip. "Is your mama finally home?"

Joey's smile broadened. "Mama's home." He turned and pointed toward the new window.

Devon turned to Neely. "I bet she's happy to be here. How's it going?"

"She's nervous, but we all said we'd help as much as we can." She gave a shrug. "I tried to get her to stay at Dad's, but she's determined to be here, so…"

"Ashley? Determined?" Devon gave a chuckle. "The little time I've known her, it doesn't surprise me."

Neely's face brightened. "Me neither. My sister is strong willed." She gestured toward the door. "Would you like to stop in and say hi? I'm sure she'd like to see you."

He turned toward Kaylee. "What do you say?" A scowl had grown on her face, and he realized her attention was pinned on Joey. "This is Joey, Kaylee. His mama just got home from the hospital. She—"

"Why are you holding him?" Her scowl deepened.

Her reaction surprised him. Devon gave Joey a little squeeze and lowered him to the ground. "There you go, big boy."

Joey tilted his head upward. "I'm a big

boy." He wandered closer to Kaylee and studied her bicycle. "Ride?"

Kaylee gave him a look. "No. This is my bike."

Devon's chest constricted. "Kaylee, don't be mean. He has his own tricycle." He'd never expected her to act rudely to Joey or anyone.

She grasped his pant leg and gave a pull. "Daddy, let's go. You're supposed to walk with me."

Embarrassed, he gave a shrug. "I'd better pass on your invitation. Tell Ashley hi from me. I'll catch her later."

Neely nodded as if she understood. He tousled Joey's hair, gave a wave and guided Kaylee back to the sidewalk, disappointed with her behavior as well as his hopes that she and Joey might become playmates. He didn't know what triggered her attitude, but he had to say something to Kaylee and get to the bottom of her reaction.

Ashley watched out the window as Devon walked away. She'd hoped Neely would invite him in, but apparently she hadn't thought to. Devon wouldn't ask, not with his little daughter with him. She released a sigh and sank back into the recliner. The little girl had dark hair like her daddy, but other than that, she couldn't see her well enough through the window to catch a resemblance. Mainly she noticed her scowl. Not a good sign.

Devon had offered to help out with Joey, and she'd hoped the kids might be friends, but the frown doused her hope. But she decided not to jump to conclusions. The look may have been caused by anything. Kids didn't like not getting their way.

What difference? Life went on. She had no expectations of anything from Devon. A small seed of anticipation had settled in her chest when he'd visited in the hospital. A neighborly friend sounded like a positive step forward, but she had the Wellses next door. In a pinch, they might keep an eye on Joey. Still, she enjoyed Devon's company except for the buzz of guilt that lingered in her brain. Though the feeling was ridiculous, her heart didn't listen to her brain. She couldn't control how she felt.

The yard looked strange without the big

tree that shaded it, but without it, more sunlight flooded the room. Sunny days were good. She needed cheering up now. She eyed her cast, her mind flying back to that fateful day when she stepped outside, only to change a piece of her life for an irritating piece of time.

But the memory sent a surprise grin. The one good moment was looking into the eyes of the man who came to her rescue. Devon's scruffy jaw settled into her thoughts. She liked how he looked. The whiskers made him appear rugged—strong and capable. A lumberjack type ready to fell trees to save her. But then, in truth, he would have to be tough and competent with the dangerous career he had. Her smile faded.

Outside, she watched Neely and Joey in the front yard. He had found something, and when she looked closer, she spotted him dangling a wiggling worm. Little boys were entertained by the craziest things. Her gaze lifted to Adam's photograph on the table. He would miss all those moments as her son matured and grew. She closed her eyes, willing away the tears and searching for a smile. If only they came more easily when she thought of Adam.

Moments later, Joey's voice piped into the living room, and she heard the door close and footsteps. She watched the archway, waiting for her sister to join her. Joey bounded in before she did, brandishing the worm.

"Look." He stuck it close to her face.

She eyed the wiggly creature. "You found a worm."

"Worm." He held it closer, studying it before he lowered his hand. "Keep it."

"No way, kiddo. That goes back outside." Where was Adam when she needed him? She lifted her head and grinned at her sister. "Give it to auntie."

Neely stepped back. "I don't want that thing." She gave her a playful frown. "He wanted to show it to you."

"Okay, I saw it." She eyed Joey. "Take the worm outside and put it on the ground. It has to go home."

"Go home?" He looked thoughtful.

"Come with me, Joey." Neely beckoned, and they returned to the backdoor.

Ashley couldn't help but grin at her son's antics. Adam would have loved it.

When Neely returned, Ashley asked the question that had lingered in the back of her mind. "Why didn't you invite Devon in?"

Her sister looked surprised. "I did. I think he started to, but the little girl tugged at him to walk." She lifted her shoulders and dropped them. "So he walked." She slipped onto the sofa. "I think she's a bit spoiled... or else she has a bad case of jealousy."

The comment bewildered her. Jealous over what? "Why?"

"I suppose she didn't like Devon's attention to Joey."

"Really." Her heart sank.

"What else? The frown appeared when Joey reached toward Devon to pick him up." She scooted back against the cushion. "He did, and I noticed her expression."

"Hmm?" Jealousy. "Maybe it makes sense, but..." She tried to put herself in the girl's place. Kaylee only had a few days to be with her dad, and sharing him wasn't part of her plans. "I'd hoped she might be a friend to Joey. We don't have a lot of kids on the block."

"You can't force friendship. Give them time. She may come around."

"Maybe." But maybe not. There was a year difference in age. She'd hoped that wouldn't be a problem. Sadly, it meant her friendship with Devon may have to be on the non-Kaylee days. Or not at all.

The light coming through the window dimmed, and she looked out at the cloud-covered sun. Her optimism had faded as quickly as the sunny day.

Devon watched Kaylee work her puzzle and pondered how to talk with her about her behavior. He'd avoided the discussion when they left Ashley's since her reaction had been a surprise. He wanted to learn why she'd behaved as she did. He'd tossed the topic around in his head as they walked and more since they arrived home, but he still hadn't settled on how to approach the topic.

He'd noticed Neely's car no longer stood in the driveway, which probably meant Ashley was alone, struggling to do things on her own. He envisioned the difficulty of handling a toddler without having two good arms and hands to use. He longed to help her but not until he could resolve the situation with Kaylee.

He shifted his thoughts back to finding the right words to begin the conversation. Without a clue, he rose and settled on the floor beside her. "You're doing a good job."

She nodded. "This one's easy."

"Maybe we should buy some harder ones since you're growing up so fast."

This time she tilted her head and grinned. "I am. I'm not a baby like that little boy."

Her comment hinted at the problem and also opened the door. "Joey's not exactly a baby. He's a smart boy and not even a year younger than you."

"But why did you hold him?"

A frown darted to his face, but he managed to soften it. "You didn't like me to hold him?"

"You don't hold me."

Devon tousled her hair, but his heart grew heavy. "That's because you're so grown up, but I could, you know." He shot up and slipped her into his arms and spun around.

Her giggle sailed to the ceiling and bounced against the walls.

Kaylee smiled so rarely in the past days, and the sound brought him peace. "See? You're not so big I can't. I didn't think you wanted me to hold you."

She hugged him around the neck. "I don't, but you shouldn't hold strangers."

Her feelings became a neon sign flashing through his head. She was envious of his attention to Joey. Wasn't he spending enough one-on-one time with her? "He's not really a stranger to me, Kaylee. Maybe I should tell you the story why he likes me to hold him."

After carrying her to the chair, he sat and cuddled her on his lap. "A week ago…" As he related the story of the fallen tree and Joey's fright, her expression changed to interest. When he came to the end, he gave her a hug. "So I guess when he sees me, he feels safe because I held him when he was scared." He brushed back her long hair and put his nose close to hers. "If you are ever afraid, I would hold you close and not let you go."

"Really?"

"Promise." He crossed his heart with his index finger. "Do you feel better now?"

She gave a faint shrug. "But he wasn't afraid today."

"No, but seeing me reminded him of when he was frightened." He leaned back and studied her serious face. "Maybe the next time you see him you could be a little nicer. He's a good boy and very smart."

"Can he read?" Kaylee's eyes searched his.

"I don't think so. Can you?"

She nodded, a proud tilt to her chin. "I can read my letters. A. B. C. And Aunt Renee helped me with some words."

Aunt Renee. The reference jarred him. What about Gina? He longed to ask, but he bit his tongue to keep quiet. One issue was enough for Kaylee. Her attitude toward Joey was the topic today. He gave her a hug. "I'm proud of you. Let's get some books to help you read even more. Then when you get to school you'll be way ahead of everyone."

"Okay, let's go." She slipped off his lap and gave his hand a tug.

"Not today. Right now I need to think about dinner. Aren't you getting hungry?"

She nodded. "Can I have some milk?"

"Sure can." He paused, wondering if he might be expecting too much. "Here's an idea. Let's surprise Joey and his mom and take dinner to their house after we eat."

She shrugged, but at least she didn't frown.

He rose and made his way to the kitchen. After putting milk in her glass, he set the carton back inside and stared into the meat drawer. As always he had a package of ground beef. Spaghetti was one of Kaylee's favorites. He suspected Joey liked it, too. Most kids did. If he made a pasta, he could run over a dish for their dinner tonight. He glanced at Kaylee, wondering how she'd respond this time.

He pulled the meat from the drawer, checked a cabinet for a jar of pasta sauce and came up successful. After setting them on the counter, he found an onion and dug out the frypan from beneath the stove. He liked the idea. He might even make some garlic bread with the loaf of Italian bread he'd purchased to slice to make French toast for their breakfast. A grin settled on his face as he went to work.

Chapter Five

The doorbell's ring sent Ashley's pulse on the rise. She grasped her crutches and made her way to the front door. When she looked through the peephole, her heart flipped. "Come in." She eased back to make room.

The door inched open, and Devon peeked around the corner, his smile brightening her dull day. "I brought you dinner."

"Dinner." His announcement registered surprise in her voice.

Joey rose from his pile of toys and dashed toward Devon, a big smile pulling his cherub cheeks, but with his hands full, Devon only greeted him while clutching the casserole.

"Ashley, this is Kaylee." He leaned closer

to his daughter. "Kaylee, this is Joey's mama. Remember I told you about her accident."

The girl nodded and clung to his side, a questioning look on her face.

Devon took a step into the room and paused. "I hope I'm not being presumptuous."

"Not at all. I'm surprised. But it's a nice treat." Ashley pushed the door closed with her crutch and waved him forward, wondering how Kaylee felt about the visit.

Devon stepped farther in, Kaylee quiet at his side, her eyes shifting from Devon to Joey. "In case you've already eaten, it can be tomorrow's dinner."

The unexpected visit unsettled her—though pleased her—and she found her manners. "No, I can't thank you enough. Neely spent the day bringing me home. She set some canned goods on the counter and promised a home-cooked dinner tomorrow night, so we're open for a meal."

"Great. I'll take this to the kitchen." He motioned in that direction with the casserole.

A grocery bag hung from his hand. "Spaghetti and garlic bread. Is that okay?"

"Okay? It sounds wonderful." She captured Joey's hand and gave Devon a wink. "Do you like spaghetti, Joey?"

"Sketti. Yum." His piping voice was followed by the usual grin spreading ear to ear.

Devon paused in the archway, loving the boy's smile but wishing Kaylee could look at life that way. "The food is still warm, so take a seat at the table, and I'll pop it into the microwave for a minute."

She made her way to the table with Joey and heard Devon push the timer. Her frustration mounted as she looked at his booster seat and at her hands clinging to the crutches. "Joey, I—I don't know how I can—"

"You'll need help until you can put some weight on that leg." He swooped Joey into the air and settled him in the chair. "See, that was easy."

"For you." She lowered herself to the seat and propped her crutches against the table edge. Fighting her frustration, she turned her head a moment to get a grip on her emotions.

"It's not going to be easy. But you'll learn,

and people will help." He rested his hand on her shoulder.

Warmth wrapped around her heart. Gentle, kind, thoughtful. Her mind flooded with the day they met. A horrible experience fated their meeting, and here he was again, caring enough to bring her dinner. The control she had managed earlier failed as tears dripped to her cheeks.

"I'm sorry if I said some—"

"It's not what you've said." She shook her head, seeing the concerned look in his eyes. "It's what you've done. You barely know me, and here you are with dinner and wisdom and—"

"And doing a neighborly deed." He gave her shoulder another pat. "Now, tell me where I can find dishes and silverware, and you and this young man can eat dinner."

As she directed, he pulled plates and forks from the cabinets and even thought to pour milk for Joey. "What would you like to drink? Coffee, tea, milk—"

"Water, please, with ice and maybe some coffee afterward." She motioned toward the counter. "Mrs. Wells brought over a cake."

He looked around the kitchen.

She motioned again. "It's on the far end of the counter. It's Joey's favorite. Chocolate."

"Not only Joey's." He gave a wink and proceeded to carry in the water and milk. Kaylee stayed beside him, shifting as he moved around the kitchen to keep out of his way. Finally he stopped. "Sweetie, why don't you sit, too. You can have some cake later. Okay?"

She didn't move for a moment and finally pulled herself away and slipped onto a chair as far from them as she could. She didn't make eye contact, and Ashley wasn't sure if she should try to engage her in conversation or let it go. Her motherly instinct prodded her to act. "Kaylee, do you like chocolate cake?"

The child only shrugged.

She didn't let that discourage her. "I like chocolate, but I like carrot cake even more. Have you seen it with the little carrot decoration on top?"

Kaylee nodded.

Devon slipped into the room with a pot holder for the table and set the casserole on it. He handed her a large serving spoon. "Dig in, and I'll bring in the garlic bread." He turned again to the kitchen.

Struck by how comfortable he seemed preparing her meal, she turned to Kaylee again, who didn't look at ease at all. While wishing she could get a response from the child, she shifted her attention to the pasta covered with tomato sauce and thick with hunks of ground beef. The scent rose on the air and her appetite that had been dulled awakened.

"Sketti, Mama." Joey sat with his fork standing on end against his tray.

She smiled and emptied a large spoonful onto his plate, then piled two spoonfuls on hers as Devon carried in the fragrant garlic bread.

He offered her a piece and then set the plate on the table and slipped into a chair. "I spotted your coffee so I started a short pot."

"Thanks." She struggled to pull her gaze away from his intriguing face. He wasn't what people called classically handsome, but he had pleasant features with deep brown eyes that looked into hers with a tenderness that befuddled her. His full cheekbones eased to a rounded chin with the hint of a

spooned it up, finished the bite and licked the spoon. "Yummy." He grinned.

With his focus half on Joey and half on Ashley, who seemed to savor the dessert, he managed to eat his own treat. He had to admit the sweet ice cream with the salty nuts and the creamy taste lured his taste buds in for another bite.

They made short work of the dessert, and when Joey scraped the last of the ice cream from the bowl, Devon brought a damp paper towel from the kitchen and wiped the toddler's hands and mouth, then lowered him to the carpet.

Ashley released a sigh and then chuckled.

Curious, he gave her a questioning look. "Did I do something?"

"No. Just thinking."

"I'm glad it made you laugh." He wished he could laugh more often instead of carrying the weight of the world on his shoulders. "Do you think I'm too presumptuous?"

"Why in the world would you ask me that?"

He shrugged and settled back into the chair. "I walked in as if I was invited and took over. I didn't ask if you were ready for dessert. I just made it. I should—"

"You should be who you are. That's what you should do."

"Are you sure?" He studied her face and saw only sincerity.

"Let me tell you what made me chuckle." She wiped her lips with the napkin and laid it beside the bowl.

"Tell me."

"I was thinking, except for this rotten cast and the hospital stay, I'm glad the tree fell on me. You know why?"

Puzzled, he shook his head.

"Because I met you. You're a bright light in my life—a special person. I've only known one person similar to you, and that was Adam, but I think you even top him."

Heat warmed him. "You're embarrassing me."

"It's a fact. Don't be uncomfortable. That's who you are. I love that in you, and funny, sometimes I feel as if I've known you forever."

He let her words wend their way through his mind. "That's how I feel. I've tried to put my finger on it. But what you just said is it." He leaned back in the chair, a concern inching into his mind. "I don't want to be a pest. If I overstep my welcome or anything, please say so."

"Ask Neely. I'm pretty blunt. So don't worry about that." She grinned. "Now, let's sit in the living room where it's comfortable."

He cleared the table while she settled into the recliner, and as soon as he came into the room, Joey met him with a book. "Read to me."

Ashley patted the arm of the chair. "Joey, don't bug Devon. I'll read to you. Let's get you ready for bed first."

He skittered across the room and clasped what looked like his pajamas. When he handed them to Ashley, one garment dropped to the floor.

"Can I help?" Devon retrieved the soft flannel pants and held out his hand to Joey. Ashley gave him the top, and he sat on the floor beside her chair and helped Joey into the pajamas. Red dinosaurs decorated the blue fabric.

"I bring those down in the morning to save me trips upstairs." Ashley motioned toward the staircase. "That's a trip with crutches."

"You mean, that's where you sleep?" He eyed the long staircase, wishing she had a better setup.

"I'm doing okay. Don't worry."

One slip, and she could fall. He didn't want to even think about it. "I don't like thinking of you alone here going up the stairs. Be careful. Please."

She nodded. "Okay, buddy, give Mama the book, and I'll read you the story."

Devon eyed the book in Joey's hand. *"Bunny Blue."*

Ashley gave him a sheepish look. "This was mine when I was a kid. It may have been my mother's. It was always a little beat-up, but it was a favorite."

"Interesting." He reached for it, and she put the book into his hand. He turned the book over and opened the cover. "I've never read it." He rose and settled on the sofa, keeping the book. "How about if I read it to him?"

"If you've never had the treat, go ahead. Everyone should read *Bunny Blue*. It has a message." She tilted back the recliner and watched him hoist Joey onto his lap.

Joey leaned against Devon's chest as he turned the pages and read the story of the little blue bunny who'd lost his bright pink bow. As he searched everywhere for it, Joey announced where he would look next. "You're giving the story away, pal." But Joey didn't seem to care.

As he read, Joey cuddled deeper into his arms. The feel of the hefty boy felt right and good, and he recalled when Kaylee was a toddler and how she would fall asleep in his arms. He missed those days. He continued the story. Bunny Blue finally gave up searching for the bow. Daylight was coming and the adults would awaken, so he had to return to the toy box without his bow. Sadly he climbed into the box, but before he knew it, the lid opened and his owner pulled him out. "Where's your pretty pink bow?" The bunny couldn't tell her. "There it is. Right there beneath you." The bunny laughed to himself. He'd hunted all night never realizing he'd had the pink bow all the time.

Devon closed the book, but the message

lingered in his mind. Sometimes people search and search to find their heart's desire, and all the time, it was right in front of them.

When he turned to Ashley, she gave a nod and pointed. "Joey missed the ending."

He gazed down at the boy, eyes closed, his breathing slow and even. "I did a pretty good job."

"You did, but now I can't get him up the stairs." She tilted her head.

"But I can." He lay the book on the sofa and eased up with the boy cuddled in his arms. "Remind me which way to go."

"Thanks." She gave him directions, and he climbed the stairs and found the boy's room. He lowered him into the bed, drew up the blanket and turned off the light. A small night-light shaped like a crescent moon glowed from a plug. He gazed down at Joey and thought of Kaylee. He touched the boy's soft cheek, whispered good-night and returned to the first floor, his mind wrapped around his concern once again.

"He's still sleeping." He settled back on the sofa and lifted the book. When he gazed at

Ashley, the lesson returned. Sometimes what he looked for was right in front of him.

Ashley lowered the footrest and leaned forward. "You look sad all of a sudden."

"Thinking about Kaylee. When I saw Joey sleeping, I thought about when she was little and happier. I wish she could be happy again."

"Devon, I can only imagine how difficult it is to live without her by your side." Her face filled with concern. "I thought she was just a bit unhappy because you'd brought her here, and she didn't want to come."

Her expression touched him. "No, she laughs once in a while, but not often even with me. I'm worried what's going on with her mother."

"You're really concerned?" She lowered her eyes as if in thought. "What do you think?"

He shook his head. "I don't know why I'm telling you. You have problems of your own."

"That's what friends are for."

He drew in a breath, wondering where to begin. "Gina's depression is what started it all." He told her about Kaylee's birth and the struggle she'd had until finally she'd made her decision to leave. "I know Renee, Gina's sister. She's a kind woman, but I don't want her raising my daughter, and I get the feeling that's what's going on."

"In what way?"

"When Kaylee tells me what she's learned or what she's doing, it's always about Renee. She never mentions her mother. I think that's strange, and I don't want to put her on the spot and ask. There's nothing worse than one parent grilling the kids about the other parent."

"But if you're worried, you need to learn the truth." She shook her head. "It's tough, but you need to know for your own peace of mind and Kaylee's welfare."

Her eyes sought his, and the caring look captured him. His pulse escalated, and a warm feeling slipped through his body. "I need to do something. You're right."

"Ask Renee."

His head jerked upward, surprised at what she'd said. "You read my thoughts."

"Two heads are better than one even if the idea is unspoken."

"That's the truth. I will ask Renee. That's the only way I'll know." His shoulders relaxed as his course of action soothed his worry.

"Will Renee tell you the truth?"

He nodded. "I think so. She's a good person."

She grasped her crutches and pulled herself up.

"What do you need? Let me get it for you."

She wiggled her finger toward him. "I need you."

"Me?" He pressed his palm to his chest.

She nodded, and he rose and went to her, trying to decipher what she wanted.

Clinging to the crutches, she looked into his eyes. "I want to give you a hug."

His heartbeat tripped as her arms enveloped him. A crutch dropped to the floor, but it didn't matter. He held her slender body against his, hoping she couldn't feel the pounding in his chest.

When he released her, she kissed his cheek. "Even I feel better."

He couldn't respond. No words could express what he felt.

Chapter Seven

As Devon walked home, Ashley's slender frame still warmed his arms, and though her eyes captivated him, tonight his gaze had drawn to her lips, perfectly shaped and full. And they'd been so close to his. Not wanting to go in that direction for his own good, he let the embrace fill his mind. She'd asked for the hug, something he'd longed to do more than he wanted to admit. His chest expanded, touched by her concern for him.

The same caring concern often preoccupied him. He worried about her and the crutches, especially now learning she had to ascend those stairs each day. He wished she had a bedroom downstairs, but she only had a small room she used as her office, and he knew she wanted to stay close to Joey on the second floor. The problem couldn't be resolved by him. He had to leave her in… God's hands.

For too long, he rarely thought of God, but more and more the faith he'd grown to know through Gina wove through his mind. He suspected Ashley's family went to church. He could ask her where she went and offer to take her there on Sunday.

The idea lifted his spirit, but as he approached his door, one concern came crashing down on him. Gina and her relationship with Kaylee. He'd assured Ashley that Renee would be honest. He hoped he'd been accurate. She would be loyal to her sister, but for Kaylee's sake, he hoped she would tell him the truth.

He unlocked the door, fastened it for the night and strode to the kitchen. He opened a can of cola and sank to a chair, thinking about the call he should make. Gina would be evasive, so he'd be better off talking to Renee. But how could he do that? Asking to talk with her would be a sure giveaway.

The kitchen clock hung on the wall in front of him. Eight-thirty. Was it too late to call? He drew up his shoulders, deciding the answer. He pulled his cell phone from his shirt pocket, pressed the number and heard Renee's voice. Though he wanted her to answer, he hesitated. "I hope this isn't too late, but I want to make sure I can pick up Kaylee on Wednesday."

"That's the plan. I have it on the calendar."

Her tone made him edgy. "Can I talk with Gina?"

"She's not here, Devon. Sorry, but I'll see Kaylee's ready for you on Wednesday. In the morning as usual."

"Yes, but it's late. Where's Gina?"

Renee released a stream of breath. "Devon, I'm not her secretary."

He'd sensed something peculiar in Renee's voice earlier, and now his concern deepened. Trying to be lighthearted, he probed. "Does she have a date?" As soon as the words left him, he wished he could take them back. He could have asked if she was working late, but he was almost certain she didn't work.

"She's not here. That's all I know."

He stared at the phone, wanting an answer, but he had no recourse. "Okay, Renee. I'll be there about 9:00 a.m. on Wednesday."

"Kaylee will be ready."

He pressed the end button and tossed his cell phone on the table. Renee's manner worried him. Something was going on, but he had no way of knowing unless she told him. The confidence he'd had that she'd tell him the truth faded. Gina and he were divorced. He had no control over her life. But he had a say in Kaylee's life, and if something was wrong, he should know.

He buried his head in his hands. Maybe he'd made a lot out of nothing. Gina may be dating. Maybe she found someone who met her needs. He sure hadn't. Gina needed more than he could give when her depression grew stronger. Maybe someone else could give her more.

The memory washed over him. The day the divorce papers arrived knocked him cold. He knew his work schedule provided an unsolvable problem, but he'd done everything else he could. He did housework, shopping, helped Kaylee with her needs—he'd done all he could to make life easier for Gina.

It hadn't been enough. He ran his fingers through his hair, wishing he could forgive himself for not being the person she needed. He didn't know to this day what he'd done wrong or what he lacked.

He slipped the phone into his shirt pocket, took the last swig of his cola and turned out the kitchen light. For now, he had to be the best father he could be. That's where he aimed his energy.

"Come on, Ash. I really want you to go with me to the hall. I need your opinion when I pick out the menu and the decor."

"What about Jon?" The determination in Neely's eyes signaled a battle. "He should care what they serve."

"When we started talking wedding plans, he made me promise I wouldn't drag him around picking out napkins and food." Her resolve didn't flag. "I can't do this alone."

Ashley studied her sister's face, feeling defeated. Her only tack was a threat. "I helped pick out the dresses, but now I'm a mess with this cast, Neely. I feel useless. I don't know how I'll be in August. If you want to replace me in the wedding party with—"

"Replace you? Are you crazy? You're my sister with or without a cast." She brushed away Ashley's words. "Anyway, you'll be fine for the wedding. You'll be out of that thing or at least in a walking cast by then."

Ashley listened, although her sister's assurance didn't help. "I still think I'll be a detriment. I need to do so many things for you, and I don't know that I can."

"Everyone will pitch in. Stop worrying." Neely shook her head as if Ashley's fears were unwarranted. "Can you go out with the crutches?"

"I suppose."

"Good. I planned to go Thursday. I'm taking off work that day."

Her own resolution folded. "Thursday...is okay, I guess."

"Great. We're only going to the hall." She leaned forward, a smile on her face. "I can't get married without my sister's input."

Ashley sighed at her sister's vehemence. "I'll go. Don't try to con me."

"That's what I want to hear, and I'm not conning you. I mean it." She rose and gave her a hug.

More ammunition. "Neely, I have Joey. You don't want him there to—"

"I'll see if Dad can care for Joey. We'll only be gone a couple of hours."

"Okay, but if Dad's busy..."

She brushed her words away again. "Stop with the worry. I'll call you." Neely leaned down and kissed Ashley's cheek. "I have to run. I have a million things to do." She gave a wave as she closed the storm door.

Ashley watched her slip into the car and back out from the driveway. The quiet surrounded her, and she grasped her crutches and hoisted herself up. With Joey napping, it meant time to work, so she made her way into the office. She'd figured out how to use an ottoman Devon had carried from the living room as a prop for her leg. Though a bit awkward, she could keep her leg up and still work at the computer.

Devon. She hadn't seen him again for a few days, and the same lonely feeling enveloped her. Before she met him, her life revolved around Joey and her work. She knew what to expect. Now she had to wonder…and worry.

She hated her indecision. One moment she wanted to stay clear of him before he became too important to her, and the next minute she knew it was too late. Her emotions wavered between head and heart. Head said to beware. His career was more than she could handle. Her heart said she could handle anything that was worth it. She wouldn't have given up a day of her life with Adam even though the outcome had left her heartbroken.

She stared at her computer screen, blurred by her tears of frustration. Feeling sorry for herself struggling on crutches and wrestling with indecision sank her into despondency. She didn't want to go there again and forced herself back to work, one letter after another to the list of clients. When she completed the last one, she hit the print button. The envelopes were ready so the job was nearly finished. Then on to the next task.

Using a form letter worked, but she had to address each one as if it were an original to the client. Then match the letter salutation to the correct envelope. She rose and pulled the stack of letters from the printer. As she did, the doorbell rang again. She grasped her other crutch and made her way to the door.

Before she reached the knob, the door inched open, and Devon peeked inside. Her pulse skipped seeing his face. Today his scruffy whiskers had returned, and the familiar longing to run her hand along the prickles resurfaced. Why his five-o'clock shadow intrigued her escaped her, but it did. She loved his rugged look, like a man who found life more important than a shave.

When he saw her, he smiled. "I thought I'd save you the trouble of answering." He motioned to the door. "Am I interrupting?"

"Not at all." He could interrupt her anytime. Devon made her feel a connection to the world and not just disabled, sitting alone with Joey as her main companion. Though she loved hearing him chatter, their conversation was less than stimulating.

"Why the grin?" He stood beside her, a lighthearted look on his face.

She shook her head, knowing she could never explain what his visits meant to her.

They were only darkened by the other side of her that wrestled with emotions. But today her heart won. "It's nice to have an adult to talk with. Though I will admit, Neely was here a while ago. She ignores my cast and wants me to go with her to the wedding venue."

"She values your opinion. What hall is she considering?"

"Neely already has the hall. She wants help selecting the menu and decorations—you know, linens and floral arrangements."

He raised his hands in the air. "I don't know a thing about planning weddings. I left that up to Gina."

As the name slipped from him, she watched his jaw tighten. Seeing his concern wrought hers. "Did you talk with Gina?"

"Do you have time?" He motioned to the chair.

She nodded, settled into the recliner and raised the footrest.

He backed into the easy chair and sank down. "No. I called, but Gina wasn't home. It was eight-thirty last night. That surprised me."

She tilted her head, still wondering what

in particular bothered him. "Maybe she had to work late."

"I don't think she works. She's living on child support as far as I know." His gaze drifted toward the window.

She could only speculate what worried him. "Is she seeing someone?"

"Maybe." He shrugged. "That doesn't matter. Renee's tone is what set me on edge." He explained the conversation with Gina's sister. "I think it's more than dating, or Renee would have told me. She knows I'm not trying to make amends with Gina."

"So you don't know what it is."

He faced her. "No, I don't." He lifted his shoulders. "I suppose I'm just looking for trouble."

"Maybe. Sometimes we have premonitions, but those aren't always right, either." As the words left her mouth, the phone rang. She glanced at the caller ID and saw her father's name. "It's Dad." She grasped the receiver, but instead of her dad, it was Neely.

"Dad's got plans for Thursday. He has a date with Alice."

"A date? Dad?" She chuckled. "Good for

him, but that messes up our plans. You'll have to go alone, unless you want Joey tagging along, and I know you don't."

"If it's Joey coming with us or you staying home, I'll take Joey."

Ashley knew better. Joey would be a big distraction. "Neely, you don't need me that much. Have Jon take the day and—"

"Ashley."

Devon's voice caused her to turn. She covered the mouthpiece. "I'll only be a—"

He waved his hand. "No, it's not that. If you need someone to watch Joey on Thursday, I'm off work. I'll have Kaylee, and I can certainly entertain Joey for a couple of hours."

She slipped her hand from the phone. "Just a sec, Neely." She refocused on Devon. "Are you sure? Kaylee may not be happy."

"Kaylee will be fine, and yes, I'm positive."

She tilted her head in question, but he nodded again. His offer solved the problem, and she finished her conversation with Neely, grateful that she didn't have to lug Joey to the hall. "Thanks so much, Devon. Neely is determined to drag me around with her, cast or no cast."

"Good for her. You need to get out. You've been penned up inside for too long."

"I have. Even grocery shopping is starting to sound good." The comment made them both laugh.

"Speaking of going places, I've been thinking..." Devon's face grew serious. "Do you attend a church?"

The question came out of the blue and surprised her. "I go to Abundant Grace over on—"

"I know where that is." He looked thoughtful.

"Why are you asking?"

"I need to start attending, I think. Kaylee should have a chance to learn about Jesus. I haven't been much of a churchgoer, and I know—"

"You might not be active at a church, Devon, but you exude godly behavior— kindness, goodness, faithfulness. You're a walking example of the fruits of the spirit."

"Fruits of the spirit? You see, that's the kind of thing I don't know. I learned manners from my parents. They're good people and raised me to be the same." He shrugged. "I can't take credit."

"But kind and thoughtful is who you are, with or without credit."

He lowered his head, as if uncomfortable with her compliment. "I suppose, but I still want Kaylee to learn those things, too."

Ashley understood. "You serve as a good example for your daughter, but learning the Sunday school stories and about Jesus' love for everyone is important. I think you're wise to want her to have a faith-based education."

"Would you mind if I go with you sometime?"

His request touched her. "I'd be pleased to have you join me, but I haven't been to church since this." She pointed to her cast. "It's so difficult to—"

"I'll pick you up and help you maneuver."

"I'd love that, and then Joey can go to Sunday school." Her chest tightened at the thought of Devon at her side. "Let me know when you'd like to go. Hopefully, I'll get into a walking cast one of these days and that will be easier."

He dug his hands into his pockets. "If not, I'll be there for you."

His words touched a deep spot in her heart. She lingered on his scruffy jaw, noticing the tension in his face. The conversation had drifted from his concern about Gina, and she wondered if it had been purposeful. "I don't want to stir up problems again, but we were talking about Gina before Neely called."

He gave a faint nod and stared at the carpet. "Right. I'm at a loss. If Renee won't open up, I can only accept that everything is okay, even though my gut tells me it's not."

She didn't have an answer. Nothing she could say would alter the worry she saw in his face. She recognized her own worry about things that might never happen to him. Many firefighters survived years of service without fatal injuries.

"I suppose this is a time I need to have faith." He raised his head, his gaze capturing hers.

"Without faith, I would have fallen apart with Adam's death. I survived. Yes, a bit war-torn. A bit uncertain, but I survived, and Joey and I are living a good life."

He studied her a moment before he rose. "This time it's my turn to hug you." He moved closer, his hand reaching for her.

She lifted herself on one foot, melting into his arms, nervous and uncertain, but loving the gentle feel of his strength holding her close. When she raised her eyes, she observed a look of longing on his face. Fresh hope charged through her with each pulse beat.

His lips eased closer, and though she wanted to step back, her heart didn't let her move. When his mouth touched hers, warmth filled her chest as she leaned into the tender kiss. His soft lips moved against hers before he eased back with a sigh.

They looked at each other a moment before reality set in. He helped her safely to the chair and stood above her, wearing an expression she didn't know how to read.

He finally spoke. "I believe this is the time I should say I'm sorry." His gaze lingered on hers.

Her emotions darted from joy to alarm and back as she sat, speechless.

He took her hand. "But I can't say I'm sorry, Ashley. I really can't."

She found her voice. "I don't expect you to."

They both released a sigh, and when they looked at each other, laughter bubbled from her throat.

Devon joined her. "Then I should say thank-you."

"I've never been thanked for a kiss. This is a first." And part of her wished that this was one of many firsts. "You know I think the world of you. I love your company, and Joey adores you."

"Do I hear a but?"

She nodded. "But we both have a lot of issues that need resolving, and…"

He crouched beside her chair. "I don't want to lose your friendship over a—"

"No, Devon, I don't, either." She leaned forward and rested her hand on his shoulder. "I'm not ending our friendship. I'm reminding myself that I have things to deal with before I can…"

"Fall in love?"

"No. That's not it." She was a bit confused,

recalling her promise not to jump into a relationship that couldn't be. "Before I can make a commitment, I guess."

"I can live with that, Ashley." His hand covered hers, his finger brushing the back of her hand. "We both have problems. Let's deal with them one at a time. One day, who knows."

"One day." She shifted her other hand and rested it on his bristled cheek, feeling the prickle of his whiskers and a rush of joy. For that brief moment, she felt whole.

Chapter Eight

Devon's eyes drooped for lack of sleep, but he had no choice. Wednesday at nine he was to pick up Kaylee. He couldn't disappoint her. He'd make sure he got to bed early tonight. He'd reviewed his plan until he felt confident Renee couldn't back away from the answers he needed to hear. The only other solution was that Gina greeted him when he arrived.

He spotted the neat brick house, lawn freshly mowed and a few flowers in beds along the front. His palms grew damp as he pulled into the driveway, but he knew what he had to do. He turned off the engine and opened the car door.

As he stepped out, Kaylee came through the front doorway, her overnight bag in her hand. His mouth sagged as he watched Renee give him a wave, say goodbye to Kaylee and close the door. His arms dropped to his sides, startled at her abrupt appearance.

"Hi, sweetheart." He managed to grin at her before his attention shot again to the closed front door. "What's wrong with your aunt Renee?"

"She's late for work." She scooted past him and hurried to the passenger side.

He followed her, took her luggage and set it in the backseat, then closed the door. He stood a moment watching his planned dialogue fade into dust. Shaking his head, he walked back to the driver's seat. Before he slid inside, Renee came out the side door.

She gave him a quick glance as she swung open her car door. "I'm late, Devon. Could you hurry?" She motioned him to back up and then slipped into her car, started the engine and began a slow roll down the driveway toward him.

He thought of standing there, forcing a confrontation, but he noticed Kaylee watching him, her expression filled with confusion, and he thought better of it and slipped inside the car. He turned the key and backed into the street, pulling away as Renee sped off in the opposite direction.

When he got his wits, he managed to reach over and pat Kaylee's leg, offering her the best smile he could manage. "How was your week?"

She told him about playing with a friend down the block, having pizza for dinner one night, and detailed a TV show she'd watched on the kids channel. He only half listened, his mind reeling with his failed plan and longing to talk with Ashley about what had happened.

Kaylee stopped her chatter, and he wondered how long she had been silent. He hadn't noticed. He needed to get a grip. "What do you want to do today?"

She shrugged. "I don't know."

He didn't know either, and though he didn't have to entertain her, he had the urge to help her enjoy the time with him. His sleep could wait.

"Let's go to a bookstore and buy some new

books for you, and maybe we can find some harder puzzles somewhere."

"Okay." Her tone perked up, and he relaxed, slipping into his thoughts while she played with the radio dial, punching buttons, listening to part of a tune and trying another station.

They pulled into a mall that had both a toy store and a bookstore, and he unlocked the doors and met her on the passenger side. Inside the bookstore, she wandered from row to row, scanning the books. He studied a few, looking for ones that would help her learn to read.

"Here's one, Kaylee. I think you could sound out the words." He'd noticed the short, rhyming words. Cat. Hat. He tucked the book under his arm.

"I have this one, Daddy." Kaylee showed him a book with a monkey dressed in a birthday hat.

"Can you read that one?"

She shook her head. "Too hard, but Aunt Renee reads it to me at night sometimes before I go to bed."

Aunt Renee again. "Doesn't your mom read to you?"

She frowned a moment. "A lot of time she's sleeping."

That didn't sound good, but he knew better than to prod more. "We can buy this one." He pointed to the book he held. "So you can practice reading words."

She grinned and dived back into the other selections. After she'd decided on two more, they paid the cashier and headed for the toy store.

Inside, he located the puzzles, and once again, Kaylee studied the pictures. They discussed which ones were too grown-up and which ones would be fun but still challenging. Recalling Joey's love for puzzles, Devon shifted to another shelf that displayed ones with larger puzzle pieces, one with cartoon trucks and another with barnyard animals. Perfect. He stuck them beneath his arm, too, and when Kaylee found two she wanted, they paid and left the store.

On the way home, she flipped through the books, finding letters she knew and sounding out words as best she could. He listened, but again his concentration was on the situation with her mother. Gina wasn't doing well still. He'd hoped she would improve during the time she'd been living with her sister. She'd resided away from their home nearly three years, living with Dwight and Renee out of the goodness of their hearts. He'd hoped life would get back to normal for Gina and for Renee. Her husband had to be a saint.

When he arrived home, Devon knew he needed to get out of the funk he was in. Kaylee lived with a mother who spent days bound by depression. She didn't need a father who couldn't enjoy life.

Kaylee opened a puzzle and emptied it on the floor. While she was occupied, he headed for the bathroom to wash his face and hands. He needed to wake up and be a fun dad. His mind clicked with possibilities and, of the options, he chose one Kaylee would like. He headed for the kitchen and pulled out a cookbook. He had only one, and it looked new. His cooking was mostly limited to frozen dinners heated in the microwave, although he had to admit his homemade spaghetti had been quite awesome.

He found a recipe and dug around the cabinets for the ingredients—flour, sugar, cocoa, shortening. Surprised, he even found a can of baking powder. He avoided checking the expiration date. Gina may have purchased it years ago.

Before he found the measuring cups, Kaylee bustled into the kitchen.

"This one's a good puzzle, Daddy." She nestled beside him, eyeing the counter to see what he was doing.

He searched in a drawer for cups. "Why is it good? You like the picture?"

"It's harder, but I can do it, I think." She gave him a quizzical look. "What are you making?"

"A surprise."

"For me?" Her eyes lit up.

"Sort of, but you're here now, so it's not much of a surprise." He tickled her side, and she jumped.

"What is the surprise?" She slipped the flour bag closer and tried to sound out the word.

"What's your favorite treat?"

"Hmm?" She tilted her head the same way

he'd seen Ashley respond. "Cookies to dunk in milk."

"I'm making you milk." He gave her a wink.

"No, you're not, Daddy. That's silly. Cows make milk." She sent him a huge grin that warmed his heart. "You're making me cookies."

Hearing her cheerful voice filled him with pleasure. Why couldn't he be playful like this all the time? "I guess it's no longer a surprise, is it?"

"I don't care 'cuz you're making my favorite." She turned the sugar bag around and pointed to the letters. "*S. U. G. A. R.*"

"Right. That's *sugar.*" He sounded the letters as he pointed to each one.

"Sugar." She mimicked him, pointing and sounding the word. When she finished, her interest returned to the baking. "Can I help?"

He envisioned the mess, but it would be worth it. He'd never tried baking with her, but she wasn't too young to learn. He gave her a hug before finding a clean dish towel, tying it around her waist and getting a stool from the hall closet. "Now you're ready."

He helped her measure and let her mix. As the batter plopped out, he scooped the misplaced ingredients from the counter and returned them to the bowl. Concentration showed on Kaylee's face, and he almost laughed as she frowned and pursed her lips, engrossed in the task.

Once the cookies were in the oven, Kaylee sat at the table and stared at the oven window anxious to taste her first baking attempt. When she asked for a glass of milk, he sat one in front of her, and then provided a sandwich of chicken with mayo. He joined her, eating one, too. As they ate, the buzzer sounded, and he managed to waylay her from dropping her sandwich and pulling out the cookies to cool. When he finished, he joined her again.

She stretched her neck and peeked at the counter as if she could see whether or not they had cooled. "Are they done now?" He gave up and slipped a warm cookie onto a napkin and set it in front of her. She grasped it, dipped it into the milk and proclaimed it the best cookie of her life.

Devon watched her, thrilled at her jubilance. Today he realized making her day enjoyable with simple activities, even lessons in baking, could uplift them both. "What do you say we take some cookies to Ashley's house and give the puzzles to Joey. Can we do that?"

She thought a minute. "Can I tell them I baked the cookies?"

"You sure can."

She nodded in agreement and as she finished the cookie, he packaged some of the treats and rounded up the puzzles for Joey. He'd learned from today. He hoped the positive attitude stuck with them both. He found it too easy to slip into the doldrums.

Ashley's pulse skipped when she noticed Devon and Kaylee heading up her sidewalk. She hadn't seen him since the kiss, and since then, her concern had multiplied. She liked him, admired him and cared, but…every day that passed without hearing from him sent off an alarm. Had he been injured or worse? No one would think to let her know. Why would they? The situation confused her.

Joey adored him, and Devon would make a perfect father. Kaylee needed affection, a life that had rhythm and solidarity, a marriage would give the little girl a more secure feeling, based on what she'd learned about Gina's instability.

But…

The doorbell's jangle was followed by Devon's voice calling through a gap in the doorway.

"Come in." Her pulse skipped as he entered. Kaylee slid in beside him, and instead of the girl's usual cautious look, her expression seemed more open. "How are you, Kaylee?"

"Fine." She glanced at her dad, then grinned. "We brought you a present."

"You did?"

The child nodded and reached up for the package Devon held along with a paper bag with a toy store logo. Something for Joey, she suspected. Kaylee carried the package to her and waited as she opened the sack and pulled out the container of cookies.

"Did you buy me cookies?" Ashley knew

they were homemade and suspected the child had helped make them.

"I baked them myself." She glanced again at her dad, who grinned but slipped in an unnoticed shrug.

"By yourself. Wow. Can I try one?" She lifted the lid while Kaylee encouraged her to take a bite. She did, letting the girl see how much she liked them. "These are the best cookies I've ever had."

"I know." Pride filled her face.

Devon gave her a poke. "You should say thank-you for the compliment."

She gave him another look, longer than the last. "Okay." She turned to Ashley. "Thanks."

"You're welcome." She lowered the container. "Would you like one?"

Devon gave her an approving nod, and Kaylee grasped a cookie and took a bite.

Before Ashley could get the cookies into the kitchen, she heard Joey's call from the second floor. "He's awakened from his nap. It's about time or he won't sleep tonight."

Devon motioned to the staircase. "I can get him for you."

"Would you?" Relieved she didn't have to maneuver the staircase again, she gestured for him to go ahead. As he ascended the stairs, she rested her hand on Kaylee's shoulder. "Want to come to the kitchen with me? You can tell me how you made the cookies."

"Okay." Kaylee followed her into the kitchen, walking as slowly as she did on crutches.

Ashley's heart stirred, witnessing the girl's eagerness to talk about her cookie-making. Such a simple activity but one that she'd enjoyed. If only Devon could find more ways to include Kaylee in his life. Seeing the child at ease lifted Ashley's spirit. She listened as Kaylee described the measuring and stirring. She did admit her daddy helped when she slopped the dough, and Ashley chuckled and said she'd done that, too. By the time Kaylee had moved on to the shopping spree with her daddy and the new books and puzzles they'd purchased, Devon reappeared carrying Joey.

As soon as he spotted Kaylee watching him, Devon set Joey down and shifted to Kaylee where he gave her a wink. "We have a present for Joey, too."

Joey's attention perked. "Present."

Devon nodded. "I set it on the chair in the living room. Kaylee, will you get it and give it to Joey?"

She skipped off and Joey pattered off behind her. In a moment, he returned with jigsaw pieces in his hand. "Puzzles, Mama."

"Your favorite. That's a nice gift." Kaylee carried in the box lid and Ashley eyed the photo. "And it's trucks. Can you make it so we can see?"

"Kaylee can help." He looked at her, and Kaylee seemed pleased.

The children trotted back to the living room, and Ashley motioned to a chair. "Have a seat. I was making a cup of tea. Would you like one?"

"Sure. Any kind. I'm not a connoisseur of tea." He gave her a wink.

Though he looked pleasant enough, she spotted something in his eyes. Curious, she poured water over two tea bags and slipped a cup in front of him with a saucer between them for the used bags. "Anything new? Did you talk with Renee?"

Devon glanced toward the doorway, apparently making sure Kaylee wasn't within earshot, and told her what had happened when he picked up the little girl.

"Do you think Renee was really late or being evasive?"

"Maybe a little of both. I didn't arrive until a little after nine. I don't know what time she starts work, but she didn't give me a moment to speak." He ran his fingers through his hair and looked off in the distance. "I'm not certain what to think."

"I'm sure it worries you."

"Kaylee told me how Renee reads to her when she goes to bed." He frowned and dipped the tea bag up and down in the hot water. "I asked if her mother reads to her."

"What did she say?" She watched him dunk the bag over and over.

"She said her mother was usually sleeping."

Ashley pressed her lips together, controlling the concerns that raced through her mind. "You wanted to hear good news, I know."

He glanced toward the doorway again. "Kaylee looked on edge when she answered me. I'm wondering if Renee is dictating how she should respond to my questions."

"Would she do that?" She hoped not, but the same thought had crossed her mind.

"A few days ago I would have said no, but now...I'm not certain." He settled the tea bag onto the saucer. "I know one thing. I need to get to the bottom of the situation, and I don't want to make an issue of it with Kaylee. It puts me in a bad position."

"I know, Devon." She reached across the table and grasped his hand, remembering after she did that she'd decided to steer clear of intimacies.

He weaved his fingers through hers and squeezed. "I need God's help with this one."

"You do, and I'll add it to my prayers. The answer will come."

They sat in silence a few moments while she listened to the children's voices, pleased that they were getting along.

Devon shifted in the chair. "Thanks for listening."

She squeezed his hand and unwound her fingers to pull the bag from her tea. "There's one positive thing I can say."

He gave her a faint smile. "I could use that."

"Kaylee looked so happy when she arrived today. It's wonderful to see. Whatever you've done to make it happen is great."

"Thanks. I had to remember to be happy, and it just followed."

"Great. Keep it up."

As his tension seemed to fade, the silence wrapped around her like a comfortable blanket.

In the living room the children talked about storybooks. She guessed Kaylee was telling Joey about the new books her dad had purchased. Their voices faded a moment until Joey's voice soared through the doorway. "My mama reads me bedtime stories."

"So." Kaylee's tone had an edge. "Mine will, too, when she gets home."

Devon's head shot up, staring at the doorway, then whipped his neck toward her, his eyes wide. "Did you hear that?"

She nodded. "God answers prayer quickly sometimes."

"I knew something was up." He closed his eyes and drew in a ragged breath. "Now I have something solid for Renee. She can't deny the truth this time."

"Will you say anything to—"

He shook her head. "No. Nothing to Kaylee."

"Good." Her heart ached for his situation. Seeking the truth when no one wanted to be open destroyed relationships and ruined trust. "Renee will be honest this time, Devon."

"She has no choice."

He leaned back in the chair, his gaze in the distance, his thoughts far away.

She remained silent and said a prayer, thanking God for answering her unspoken prayer and asking Him to bless Devon with peace of mind.

Devon sat in front of the TV, fighting his desire to get more details from Kaylee but knowing it wasn't the right thing to do. What surprised him was, if her mother wasn't home, why hadn't Kaylee mentioned it? Saying she missed her mother or some other comment seemed a typical thing for a child to say, even offhand.

At least now he could confront Renee, but if Kaylee didn't get to bed soon, it would be too late to call. He eyed his watch and headed for the dining room.

Kaylee sat at one end of the table, a puzzle spread out and the picture starting to take shape. He ambled toward her and studied the pieces. If he found a few, he could hurry her.

But when he spotted a possibility and reached for it, she tilted her head and frowned at him. "Don't do my puzzle, Daddy. I want to do it myself."

Surprised at her admonition, he withdrew his hand and pointed to his watch. "It's time for you to be heading for bed."

"Can't I finish?" She drew back and pointed to the portion she had left. "I'm almost done."

"You can finish it tomorrow. That will be fun."

"No, it won't." The frown he hated to see deepened.

He struggled for a response. "Bed now, and we can start one of your books."

"You'll read to me?" Her face brightened.

"For a little while. Okay?"

She slipped sideways in the chair and stood. "Okay, but not just for a minute."

He grinned. "Longer than a minute."

She accepted that and skipped into her room. Within minutes, he heard her running water in the bathroom and was pleased she voluntarily brushed her teeth each night without a reminder. Someone had taught her that lesson well.

When she called for him, he strolled in, hoping to hurry the process but not wanting to rush too much. "Want to read one where you can sound the words? Or how about *Miss Lina's Ballerinas?*"

"I never heard that one before." She snuggled into the blanket, and he propped himself beside her, his feet dangling over the edge. He held the book low so she could see the pictures and began reading her the story about eight little girls who studied dance with Miss Lina. Devon chuckled himself when he saw their names. "Listen to their names, Kaylee. Ready?"

She nodded, and he began. "Christina, Edwina, Sabrina, Justina."

Kaylee started to giggle.

He loved hearing her happiness. "There's more. And Katrina, Bettina, Marina and Nina."

The laughter made his heart burst, and he continued the story of the young girls who danced while reading and doing schoolwork, in the park, and… "Kaylee, do you know where else they danced?"

She shrugged, her eyes getting heavy.

"They danced into bed." He chucked her under the chin. "And that's what you're doing right now. Dancing in your dreams." He slipped off the mattress and kissed her cheek. "Good night, sweetheart."

"Night, Daddy." She didn't open her eyes, but a faint smile stole to her lips.

His chest tightened realizing the mistake he'd made for so long. He'd allowed his concern to seep into her mind. Children weren't dumb. They sensed things the same as adults. They just didn't know how to process it. He thanked the Lord for the awareness.

He set the book on her lamp table and made his way to the door, turning off the light. In the hallway, he breathed a sigh and checked his watch. Still early enough to call Renee.

After filling a glass with milk, he settled in the living room, then pulled out his cell phone and pressed in the number. It rang four times before someone picked up. He feared it would be Renee's husband, Dwight, but she finally said hello. It dawned on him, she had caller ID and had probably considered not answering.

"Is something wrong with Kaylee?" Her voice edged with tension.

"No. She's fine, Renee. I'm sorry to call late, but I wanted to tuck Kaylee in first."

Silence.

He gathered his thoughts. She suspected something.

"What's this about?" Her question sounded tenuous.

"It's about Gina. Where is she, Renee?" His palm felt damp against the phone. "Don't play games with me, please. Just tell me the truth."

"Did Kaylee say something to you?"

"No, but why shouldn't she?" The truth struck him, and his anger rose. "Did you tell her not to tell me? Is that it?"

"If she didn't say something, how do you know Gina's not here?"

His fingers gripped the phone as tight as a vise. "Did you tell Kaylee not to say anything to me?"

"Yes, Devon. I did."

He boiled. "Don't ever do that again to my daughter. Don't ever put her in a position to lie to me or hold problems back. I won't stand for it."

"Face facts, Devon. I'm raising your daughter because her mother's incapable, and—"

"Hold on." *Incapable.* The word smacked him. "What do you mean incapable?"

"I don't have to tell you. Gina's had problems for years and it's only gotten worse."

"Where is she now?"

"Hospitalized from a prescription drug overdose."

His gasp reverberated into the phone. "Why didn't you tell me? Why keep it a secret?"

"Gina doesn't want to worry you."

"Or stir up trouble. Isn't that closer to the truth?" His body trembled with frustration.

"Probably."

Confusion and concern knotted in his chest. He needed to think. He needed to act.

"Devon, don't do anything drastic. Kaylee's fine with us, and I know your work schedule isn't conducive to caring for her full-time."

His schedule was a convenient excuse but not anymore. "I need to think, Renee. Let's drop this for now, and I'll get back to you." A new thought slipped into his mind. "Will Gina be all right?"

"This time."

The answer struck him like a steamroller. "I'm glad. I'll talk to you later, but please don't put Kaylee in that situation again. It's not fair to her to keep secrets from me."

"I'm sorry. I was following Gina's request."

"You're the healthy one. Gina isn't. Do what you know is right."

"I will."

He thanked her and hung up, his body

quaking with shock. He had a problem to solve. Kaylee deserved a whole parent, one who loved her with all his heart. He had to act now.

Chapter Nine

Ashley maneuvered her crutches through the hall doorway while Neely held it open. Devon had picked up Joey as promised, but hadn't had the opportunity to tell her what he'd learned about Gina with the kids present. She was eager to hear what had happened.

"Thanks." She swung her leg forward as they made their way toward the office door. On her way, she'd noticed two large banquet rooms, both with lovely chandeliers hanging from the ceiling, large round tables and a wall of windows looking out to the setting beyond.

Neely pointed. "The hall looking into the garden is ours."

Admiring the view a moment, Ashley shifted forward and looked into the second room. The setting through the window appeared to be a patio with a large fountain, today not spouting water, but she assumed it did for varying events. She agreed with Ashley's choice, preferring the garden that would be a lovely summer setting.

A woman appeared from the office, her hand extended. "Neely Andrews, I assume. I'm Jessica Rushford."

Neely greeted her and introduced Ashley. She beckoned them back into the office. "Let's talk menu first and then decor."

Ashley heard them talking and tried to wrap her mind around the menu, but the details escaped her. Instead, her thoughts were on Devon, the double problem. The first was Devon's situation with Gina and getting the details of her absence from Renee. The second problem was her own. How could she stop herself from falling in love with a man she could never marry?

Then she considered Joey. Devon had won the boy's heart without trying. He'd learned Devon's name although she never knew how it would come out. Joey often said Debon. It made her chuckle.

Chicken with artichokes and capers. The dish brought her back to the task at hand. She forced her attention to the conversation.

"What do you think, Ash?"

She eyed Neely, having no idea if she was talking about the chicken or some other dish. "Everyone likes chicken."

"No, I meant the stuffed pork loin. That's different." Neely pointed at the banquet menu. "Or we could go with the beef." She curled her nose.

The look gave Ashley the clue. "Pork is different. Everyone has beef."

"Good. That's what I thought."

As Neely settled on the potato dish, vegetables and salads, Ashley sailed back to her own quandary. Could she and Devon remain friends? No more touches. Avoid the looks that became kisses. Could she do it?

Why not? She could if she wanted to avoid his romantic overtures, but that's the question she couldn't answer. The look in Devon's eyes drew her in and tangled her in threads of longing. Being touched, feeling a man's hand on hers, his arm embracing her, the feel of his lips against hers, she'd missed those feelings since Adam flew off for duty. She'd almost forgotten how amazing it had been wrapped in the feelings of being special and loved.

Not that she knew Devon loved her. The question jarred her mind. He was caring and tender. Was his kiss one of romance or one of...? Why did she try to fool herself? She could tell a friendly peck on the cheek from a kiss that held promise. Devon had feelings for her. She didn't know the depth, but she knew they were real. And if she were honest, so were hers.

"Ash."

Her head twisted toward Neely, hoping her eyes didn't look as glazed as they felt. "What?"

"You're here to help me. I don't think you're listening."

"I am...sort of. My mind wandered for a minute." Ten minutes. Maybe fifteen.

Her sister shoved a paper into her hand. "Look at this. What do you think?"

She scanned the wedding menu—traditional appetizers of veggies and dip, cheese and crackers, with entrées the two meats she'd discussed with Neely, potatoes au gratin, mixed vegetables, a variety of salads, dinner rolls and a buffet of minidesserts. "It looks wonderful. I wouldn't change a thing."

"Naturally we'll have a wedding cake, too." Neely took back the menu and handed it to Jessica. "And a punch to be served with the appetizers."

"Certainly." Jessica made a note on the paper. "That's a given, but you can have a fruit punch with sherbet or one that's less fruity that the gentlemen usually prefer."

"That would be fine. We need to please everyone."

Ashley agreed, mainly to let her sister know she'd been listening. She had to stay focused.

"Now, I'll prepare a copy of this for you while you and your sister look through this album that shows the available colors for the linens and some of our table centerpieces." She rose, set the album on the table beside them and left the room.

Neely opened the cover, but instead of

looking at the pictures, she shook her head and stared at Ashley. "What's wrong with you? You're off in Wonderland."

"No, I'm...I'm just—"

A concerned look flew to Neely's face. "I'm so sorry. I didn't think when I asked you to come that you might think back to your own wed—"

"Neely, no." She touched her sister's arm. "It's not that at all. My mind is on a multitude of things, but mainly my relationship with Devon."

"What happened? Did he do something to—"

"Nothing. He did nothing." Other than kiss me. "It's me. He's wonderful, and I like him more than I can say, but I can't get involved with him. I can't let myself do that. I'd hurt him and myself because no matter how much I'd like to, I can't form a relationship with a man whose job puts his life in danger daily. I can't."

"Did he lead you to believe he wants more than a friendship?" She slipped her hand on Ashley's shoulder. "I know he's around some, but maybe he's just lonely and wants a friend."

"That's what I told myself until..."

Neely's eyes widened. "What? Until what?"

Ashley knew she'd blown it, and she didn't have time to discuss the whole thing before Jessica came back. "Let's look at the album. We can discuss this later."

"Until what?" Determination glinted on Neely's face.

"He kissed me."

"He did?"

The memory washed over her. "And I kissed him back."

Neely sat unmoving for a moment. "I can't say I'm not glad, Ash. He's a really nice guy, and I want you to find someone in your life who can fill the emptiness you've felt since the tragedy with—"

"And live day in and day out waiting for another person to come to my door and tell me my husband died trying to save someone's life." No matter how she fought her emotion, tears blurred her vision. "I can't do it."

Neely's hand grasped hers. "Ash, I—"

"How are you doing, ladies?" Jessica's voice pierced the conversation.

"Sorry, we got sidetracked." Neely chuckled. "You know, two sisters with a million things to talk about." She turned to Ashley. "Let's finish this so Jessica can get back to work." She shifted the album so they could both see it and discussed color scheme.

Ashley did her best to focus. They could talk later, but the problem was hers, and all the talk in the world couldn't change a thing.

Devon watched Kaylee crouch through the colorful tunnel of tubes and head for the slide. Joey followed. He loved seeing the two children play. Today Kaylee had behaved like a big sister.

He'd decided a fast-food treat with a play area would help pass the time and keep them entertained. He didn't realize how entertained he would be watching them. Having fun had escaped him for too long. He hadn't realized until Ashley came into his life. She'd become his fresh air, one without smoke and danger. A life with smiles and laughter, with spontaneous moments. One with a kiss he longed to repeat.

Ashley's comments of friendship, not commitment, concerned him, though he understood and agreed. They both had issues. He needed to resolve the situation with Gina. He wanted the truth, and Ashley longed for something, but a something he couldn't put his finger on. Some days he sensed Ashley still loved her husband so much that she couldn't release the devotion and look ahead at life. Other times, he tossed out the idea. She had grown beyond that, although she would never stop loving his memory. He admired that. It meant she'd found a true love and for some reason the Lord had chosen to take that love from her.

But for what? Was it for him? Would God do that? The idea seemed ludicrous. War wasn't God's doing. Evil caused war. Selfish, immoral individuals wanting what didn't belong to them, striving to stamp out lives they didn't value. That wasn't God's doing. He preserved life so it could be abundant. He remembered hearing that in church years back with Gina. He liked the idea of an abundant life. Not money. He knew it wasn't that kind of abundance, but an abundance of joy and health and well-being serving the Lord and praising Him. Walking in His steps.

He'd forged his own trail, and time had come to detour back to the path set for him. What that plan was he didn't know, but he wanted to trust. He wouldn't have Kaylee over the weekend, but he wanted to attend worship anyway.

When Joey wanted to play in the bin of colorful balls—a sea of color that rolled and pitched like waves, Kaylee said she'd rather not. They shifted closer so he could keep an eye on Joey and see what was up with Kaylee. Her earlier giggles had passed, and a serious look showed in her eyes.

He sat on the edge of a nearby bench, giving a wave to Joey, but while his eyes were on him, he drew Kaylee closer. "Are you sad about something?" He glanced her way.

She gave a shrug.

Her demeanor let him know she had a problem. "Tell me what's bothering you."

"If I do, I'm doing something bad."

Her head lowered, and his heart broke. "Bad in what way?"

"Aunt Renee told me not to say stuff and I want to."

His pulse jumped, hoping. "Is it a bad word?"

A faint grin dissipated her tense face. "Daddy, I don't say bad words."

"Good. Then if it's not a bad word, you can say it if it's the truth." He gave her a squeeze. "Is it?"

Kaylee nodded. "Mommy's in the hospital."

"And you weren't supposed to tell me." He knew why, but he wondered about her understanding.

"She said so you wouldn't worry, and—" she turned to face him "—Mommy's afraid you will want me to live with you."

His chest constricted. "Would that upset you?"

"No." She slipped her arm around his back. "I want to. We have fun, and you teach me to bake."

"But life's not always fun, Kaylee. I have to go to work, too, so I'd have to have someone take care of you while I'm gone. You know I work two whole days at a time."

"Ashley could watch me." She searched his eyes.

His chest ached. "She likes you a lot, but I don't know about that. We'd have to see what we could work out."

"But maybe?"

Her desire to live with him hugged his heart, yet worry tried to pry it away. Having Kaylee live with him would be problematic. Yet it was what he wanted. Kaylee needed security and a parent's guidance. Renee had made a valiant effort, but she was an aunt not a mother or father who loved Kaylee dearly. "Let's see what happens, sweetheart."

He knew Renee would fight him, as would Gina if she knew, but Kaylee had admitted preferring to live with him, and that was all he needed to know.

Kaylee rested her cheek against his. "I love you, Daddy."

"I love you with all my heart, Kaylee." He turned his face to hers. "Thank you for being honest. Your aunt Renee shouldn't ask you to keep secrets from me. I understand why she did, but I want you to know that you can tell me anything. I won't get angry at you. We'll work things out together. Do you understand?"

"We'll work things out together." The faint smile curved her lips. "Me and you."

"Me and you." He wrapped his arms around her and held her close.

Ashley slipped from Devon's car and opened the backdoor. While Joey squirmed to get loose from the car seat, she unsnapped the belts, and he grinned. "There you go, big boy." She opened her arms and he reached for her.

Devon stepped beside her and hoisted Joey into his arms. "Where does he go for Sunday school? I'll take him for you."

She gave him directions as she hobbled on behind them across the parking lot, and before she reached the sidewalk, Devon had returned.

"No problem. Joey knew exactly where to go." He stepped beside her and moved along with her to the front of the church and up the two steps into the building.

Devon looked around as they entered, his curiosity not easy to hide. "Very nice." He pointed into the sanctuary. "I love the stained-glass windows. They're beautiful."

"I find solace in them, too. The prisms of color find their way across the seats and spread out on the carpet like a rainbow."

"Isn't that God's promise."

She grinned. "It sure is." He placed his hand on her back and avoided bumping the crutch out from under her.

He pointed to a back row. "Do you want to sit here?" His gaze shot to her crutches. "Or are you willing to tackle the walk?"

"Let's go down a ways." She started forward, and when her arms appeared to grow more weary than they were already, she stopped. "I'll sit on the end."

He slid into the second seat and reached toward her crutches. When she'd maneuvered her way into the row, he took the crutches and placed them on the floor beneath their seats. He opened the program they'd been handed by the usher and perused the inside while she watched him, wondering what he was thinking. "Have you decided what to do yet?"

His head shot up, and it took him a second to understand her question. "About Kaylee, you mean?"

She nodded. "I just wondered. I know you're thrilled that she told you the truth on her own."

"That was one of the best moments I've experienced in months with Kaylee. I can be a real dad. She not only told me what was happening but said she'd love to live with me." He shook his head. "I was so—"

"You were amazed."

"Amazed. Yes." His head lowered. "But I'm not sure what to do. What's best for her? I'm struggling with separating my heart from my brain. This decision needs wisdom, and I—"

"Devon, can't wisdom and heart be the same?" Hearing her response surprised her. She'd struggled with the head-heart battle since she'd met Devon. Maybe the two could never agree.

His head inched upward. "Maybe it can." He sat a moment, and before he said anything else, the music began and the choir filed in and settled into their seats.

She realized the conversation would continue later, but her own question stayed put in her mind. Could her emotion and her wisdom come up with the same result? Her thoughts roiled in her head until the choir opened the service. The words to the old hymn washed through the room in soft sweet lilting tones. *I need Thee, oh, I need Thee. Every hour I need Thee.* She needed help.

So did Devon. He slipped his hand over hers and gave it a pat.

His action gave her hope that he realized his need for God in his life. She kept her focus on the music and in prayer.

As the service progressed, the theme for the day came to life in the opening song. Then the pastor spoke on the need for the Lord's guidance and love, and the way to receive it was through trust.

Awareness swept over her. She lacked trust and not only trust in God, but trust in everyone. She lived on the fringe of fear, and it was no way to live. In fact, it wasn't really living. The meaning rolled through her, leaving her searching for ways to overcome her present view of life.

As the service reached its close, the congregation stood for the final prayer. She remained seated, not wanting to balance on one foot, but Devon rose, sending her a smile and a nod. After the prayer, the congregation agreed in a final Amen, and the pastor lifted his arms. "Remember these words from Proverbs 3:5-6. "*Trust in the Lord with all your heart and lean not on your own understanding; in all your ways acknowledge him, and he will make your paths straight.*' Now, go in peace."

The choir rose and sang its final song, the music a backdrop for her thoughts. The simple words from Proverbs covered her with a kind of peace she hadn't felt in a long time. She had to trust the Lord with all of her being and not try to make sense of life on her own. If she trusted fully, the Lord would guide her.

When she opened her eyes and lifted her head, Devon stood as if transfixed. She needed her crutches, but she didn't want to disturb him. She longed to know where his thoughts lay.

The anthem ended and the choir filed out in the hum of conversation as worshippers made their way toward the door. Devon looked at her, a smile easing to his face. He didn't ask but bent to retrieve her crutches. As she put them beneath her arms, his hand rested again against her back as if supporting her.

She inched her way out of the pew and into the aisle where people she knew greeted her and asked about her health.

Devon paused with her until she had a moment free and then he motioned toward the side door. "I'll go that way and collect Joey, okay?"

"Good idea." She nodded to the people. "I'm like a snail here."

"Don't rush. I'll meet you at the front."

He hurried away, and her spirit lifted. Maybe the head and heart could come to an agreement if she could hang on to trust and faith.

If. Why had she used the word? She could

never move ahead while she continued to question herself. *Lord, I need You. Oh, I need You.*

Devon hooked Joey into his car seat, making sure the belt was secure before turning his attention to Ashley. She slipped onto the seat, using her crutches as a prop while she swung in her legs. He chuckled. "You're becoming quite proficient with those crutches."

"It's that or scream." She tilted her head and sent him a silly grin. The sunlight glistened on her hair falling in a cascade around her shoulders, and golden highlights glinted in the sea of mahogany.

His fingers twitched to weave through the soft curls. He closed the passenger door and hurried around the car, sending his thoughts deep into his mind. She'd stated her feelings. Friends only. Her declaration rang like a punishment and not a promise of possibilities.

He slid into the driver's seat, took a final look at Joey playing with a miniature car he'd found tucked into the seat and headed toward the highway. The pastor's message had lightened his spirit and now he grappled with the issues at hand. His relationship with Ashley and his confusion over Kaylee ended the bliss he'd enjoyed.

"Devon."

He glanced toward Ashley, surprised he'd drifted so far away.

"Are you okay?"

He slipped his hand from the wheel and touched her arm. "I'm fine. I enjoyed the service and the message. It's one I needed to hear." *If only I can hang on to it.*

"Do you want to talk more about Kaylee?"

He knew she was looking at him, and though he needed to make a decision, he felt overwhelmed. "I want her to live with me. I've decided that, but first I need to search for somewhere she can stay on the days I work. It's not like a nine-to-five job. I'm gone forty-eight hours, and—"

"Would you like a suggestion?" She tugged on her seat belt and shifted in the seat to face him.

"My mother, right? I'm not sure that will—"

"Not your mother."

His chest tightened and a scowl pulled on his face. "Then who?"

"Me."

She'd been Kaylee's suggestion, but the idea had seemed far-fetched. "You're on crutches, Ashley. You have Joey, and you work, too. How can you—"

"Kaylee can take care of herself for the most part, and she'd be a help for me. She'll play with Joey and do little things that will make my life easier. I don't see it as a problem. I have an extra bedroom, too."

He weighed her words as he struggled with the "only being friends" idea. Her suggestion would bind them together more tightly. Could he keep his promise to remain friends when she'd already captured his heart? "That's asking a lot of you, and think of the...ramifications."

"What do you mean?" Her voice sounded tentative.

He figured she knew what he meant but didn't want to face it. "We're weaving our lives together. Is that what you want?"

She didn't respond, but he could see she was thinking. "It's not really weaving. It's…" She shrugged. "Kaylee will start school next year. Then she'll just spend the evenings with me."

"I'm a firefighter and always will be. It's not for a year or two. One day you'll want to get on with your life, and then—"

"This is my life, Devon. I'm Joey's mother and I work in my home. The arrangement works for me. And I'm not sure what the future holds, but—"

Her voice sputtered with emotion. He sensed tears in her eyes, and he wished he'd not started this conversation while he was driving. "I'm sorry. I was wrong." He longed to hold her, to soothe her, to understand what he'd said that triggered her frustration. How could he continue to bind up the strong feelings he had for her and not let them show? "I'll talk with Renee. I hope she agrees without an argument, but with Gina in the hospital and her health getting worse, I hope we can come to an amicable agreement without getting attorneys involved."

Ashley released a deep sigh. "Do you think it would come to that?"

"I don't know what to think anymore. I'll talk with Renee and we'll see."

Chapter Ten

"I need to talk with you, Renee." Devon swallowed his apprehension, trying to maintain calm in his voice. He knew she would balk if he came on too strong.

"Talk about what?" His mild manner didn't alleviate her uptight attitude.

"Kaylee."

"What about her?"

He wished they could talk in person, but he couldn't in front of Kaylee. Words were lost for a moment until he got a second wind. "Since her mother is hospitalized, I've decided to—"

"Gina's here, Devon. Would you like to speak to her?"

Air left his lungs. Now what? His argument failed, and yet her presence didn't change his mind. "Yes, if she's there."

He heard the telephone receiver hit something hard and Renee's voice ebbing away from the phone. Moments passed while he clung to his cell phone and reorganized his thoughts.

"Devon." Gina's voice sound feeble, no energy, no momentum. Dead.

Steadying himself, he grasped his determination. "How are you?"

"Okay."

"When were you released?"

She sighed. "I'm sorry you learned about that. It was unfortunate."

"Why is it unfortunate?" Tension knitted his body.

"You worry about things."

"Your absence affects Kaylee's life, Gina, not mine. I should know when things aren't going well for you."

"You can't do anything." Her tone heightened.

"But I can. I think Kaylee should live here with me until you're up and about. Renee shouldn't be the one raising our daughter. Not when she has a father who's willing to care for her."

"How, when you work the hours you do?" She ran out of breath. "Renee loves Kaylee, and—"

"I love her, Gina, and she loves me. She wants to—"

"No."

He pulled back the phone and peered at it. "You can't say no and think that will end it."

"But I did. No. She's staying here."

He bit the edge of his lip, holding back the frustration that raged inside him. How could she expect him to accept her no? He didn't want to drag her to court, and he knew mothers always were favored over fathers, but… His jaw tightened. "Can I reason with you? Let's make the move temporary until you're ready to be a mother to her, when you can—"

"I am her mother. I'm not listening to another word."

The clang of the receiver resounded in his ear and the hum of silence. He lowered his cell phone, hit the end button, and slipped it in his pocket as he crumpled against the chair back. What now?

What would convince her? Or would nothing result in an amicable change of custody? No matter what he did, Kaylee would be in the middle, and he never wanted to put her in that position. Her feelings outweighed winning a battle, but he wanted the best for her, too.

But what was best?

The sermon he'd heard the day before slipped into his mind. He couldn't battle this alone and the pastor had reminded the congregation that all they need do is give their problems to God and wait for His answer. *Cast all your anxiety on Him because He cares for you.*

So simple. Yet could he do it? He lowered his face in his hands and prayed.

Hearing the disappointment in Devon's voice, Ashley drew back. "Renee said no?" His shadowed jaw gave him a worn-out appearance instead of the rugged one she loved to see. He looked crestfallen.

"It wasn't Renee. Gina's out of the hospital."

The bottom fell from Ashley's stomach. "I'm so sorry it happened like this." She moved her crutches out of the way and sat on the sofa as she patted the seat beside her.

He propped the crutches to the side and sank into the cushion. "I can fight her. It's not that. But I know a fight puts Kaylee in the middle. Her mother fighting for her on one side and her dad on the other. Where does that leave her but pulled from one to the other? I can't do it." He lowered his face into his hands.

She rested her palm against his back, longing to hold him in her arms, but she'd promised herself to be more aware of her actions that encouraged romance. She couldn't guarantee anything. She had to know where she stood. What did she want? She didn't want to mislead Devon. But she didn't want to set herself up for failure. She wanted to be open to options besides the negative ones embedded in her mind.

Devon lifted his head and looked at her.

Acting on instinct, Ashley slipped Devon's hand into hers. "We both need to silence our fears and open ourselves to creative options. Open ourselves to the Lord's will."

He weaved his fingers through hers. "I know. I keep thinking of the message in church. Hope. Trust. Faith. Sometimes I can't find them. I know they're there, but—"

"But we bury them under black thoughts. The buts and ifs of our lives are our un- doing, Devon. I realize that now. When I said to you maybe head and heart can work together, I faced my actions and thoughts. Instead of saying never, we can say, it's pos- sible." She lifted her free hand and cupped his jaw, feeling a hint of bristles beneath his morning shave. "Do you understand what I mean?"

He gave a nod as he shifted his hand be- neath hers and kissed her fingers. "I do, and I agree with you. It's too easy to be nega- tive. Gina is home now, but Renee hinted that hospitalization will happen again. I as- sume it happened before except that was kept from me, too."

She lowered her hand, her heart ready to burst from her chest. "And then you can act."

"I don't wish Gina harm, but she's struggled now for years. Maybe years before she left me, and she kept that from me. It would be easy to do with my erratic work schedule. Now that I think of it, this was a possibility. It could easily be why she wanted to live with her sister. Renee knew what was going on—things I didn't know—and she wanted to safeguard Kaylee from those moments when she had little control over her emotions. That explains so much."

"I'm glad you've sorted it out. It clears up some questions I'm sure you've had these past years." She imagined where her mind would have gone if Adam had hidden problems from her. She would have blamed herself.

"I did. I faulted myself for not having what she needed, not being a good husband because of my work. The possibility that her illness drove her to Renee's, and not my faults or flaws, lifts a burden from my shoulders. It changes a lot of things."

"Focuses your perspective."

He nodded, his eyes glazed with thought. "I have a lot to rethink."

And so did she.

* * *

"When's your appointment?" Devon watched Ashley's smile broaden.

"This Wednesday and—could I hear a drumroll?—the surgeon said I might get my walking cast then." She lifted her arms and shook imaginary pom-poms.

"Congratulations." He reached over and gave her a high five. "But don't be disappointed if it doesn't happen. He said you *might*." He settled into the easy chair.

A playful scowl slipped to her face. "Don't ruin my moment. I'm confident that it will happen."

He tilted his head, wanting to tell her he hated to say I told you so if it didn't happen. "I'll hope along with you. How's that?"

"Good." She leaned back in her chair. "My appointment is on July 3, so you know what that means?"

"Hmm… Let me see. Could it be the Fourth of July?" He sent her a playful grin, happy she'd introduced the subject. "I'm off, and I'll have Kaylee. How about a picnic to celebrate? Maybe even some fireworks later."

She pointed to the cast. "Only if…" She

shrugged. "Walking through a park on crutches wouldn't be—"

"A park isn't the only place for a picnic. You've never been to my house, have you?"

Her eyes widened. "No, but I've always admired it from the street."

"Then my yard would work fine. Different for you and Joey, and convenient for both of us."

"And fireworks?" She arched a brow.

Happy she'd asked, he gave her a wink. "We can see the fireworks at Rackham Golf Course from my upstairs balcony. Comfortable seats and no crowd."

"You've thought of everything." She rubbed her hand along the top of her cast. "And if this thing is off, I'll be the best company you've ever had."

"You are anyway." When he saw a flush rise to her cheeks, his pulse skipped. She did care about him, but he longed for more. He sensed she felt the pull of attraction when they were together, but she fought it. Hiding her emotions hadn't worked. He read it in her face, and he wished he understood what she wanted to avoid when it came to falling in love.

She brushed at her cheek as if the flush were stray hairs. "If I have a walking cast, I can make it down the aisle at Neely's wedding without crutches."

The time had flown since he'd met Ashley. Sometimes it seemed like yesterday, and other times, he felt as if he'd known her forever. "Maybe you can dance at her wedding."

"I'm not sure about dancing. Walking will be enough for me." She grinned, and as her grin faded, she lowered her head. "Can you arrange a specific day off from work? I know your schedule is different from most people's."

"Usually." His pulse skipped as he anticipated her invitation. "What day in particular?"

"You know I'm asking you to be my escort for the wedding. It's August 3."

"I'd be honored to be your escort. I'll put in for the day." He sent her a wink. "Maybe even two."

She was about to respond, but the side door opened, and Joey's voice sailed from the kitchen. He whipped around the corner, and his eyes widened. "Devon."

He chuckled, hearing the boy pronounce his name correctly. He opened his arms, and Joey bounded toward him. Snatching him up, Devon twirled him around and set him down by Ashley.

"There's my boy." She wrapped him in a bear hug. "Did you and Grandpa have fun?"

Neely came through the archway and grinned. "I brought you a container of soup. I made it for Dad, and I think I have enough for a battalion." She grinned at Devon. "How's it going?"

He gave her a thumbs-up.

"Dad and Joey had a great time. The park had clowns, a guy making balloon animals, face painters, although you'll notice your son doesn't have one."

"Why not?" Ashley gazed at Joey. "You didn't want—"

He shook his head as if dislodging a bee. "For girls."

A laugh burst from Devon. "Typical boy." He recalled his own feelings as a kid. He'd been shocked when one day girls looked different to him. Much different.

Ashley and Neely covered their mouths to avoid laughing.

Ashley motioned toward the sofa. "Neely, why don't you sit."

"I can't stay, but I wanted to tell you I got a phone call from Paula and she said—"

"Paula who?"

"Our cousin." Neely rolled her eyes.

Ashley sighed. "Who else? We haven't heard from her in a long time."

"She called about her mother. Aunt Florence isn't doing well." Neely sank onto the sofa. "She and Paula didn't get along remember? That's why Paula moved out years ago, but now she's back caring for her."

Ashley shook her head. "Sounds familiar, doesn't it?"

Neely gave a nod. "Paula's call made me think about Mom's critical ways. Aunt Florence and Mom were sisters. Something rubbed off on both of them."

Uncomfortable listening to their family talk, Devon rose and moved to where Joey had dug out his toy schoolhouse and playground. Not wanting to eavesdrop, he joined Joey and put the desks into the school while Joey created a playground with the swing and slide.

Devon had been curious about their mother. Ashley didn't say much about her except her mother had died. Maybe Ashley's avoidance of relationships had something to do with her relationship with her mother. Far-fetched, but it helped having something concrete to ease his confusion.

Neely pulled keys from her pocket. "I need to go." She rose and took a step toward Joey. "Bye, sweetie." She gave a little wave and then faced Devon. "Sorry. I didn't mean to take over the conversation."

He waved her words away. "You had family business. You'll notice I've got important work here." He held up one of the plastic children and set it behind the toy desk.

Neely grinned, offered another goodbye wave and headed toward the side door.

When the side door closed, he rose from the floor, since Joey was entertaining himself, and shifted closer to Ashley. "Does this mean a visit to your aunt?"

She shook her head. "Paula suggested we wait, but I don't know. The question is, wait for what?"

Understanding her innuendo, he shook his head. "You should do what you think is right."

Her thoughtful expression ebbed. "We'll see."

Finding a way to lead the conversation into Ashley's relationship with her mother seemed pointless. He could see she'd dismissed that conversation. He slipped into the easy chair. "How will you get to your appointment Wednesday?"

"Neely's taking me. She'll go into work late."

"I'm off on Wednesday. I'd be happy—"

"You do enough for me, Devon. I've made plans with Neely."

Ashley's abrupt response threw him. Either she was irritated or distracted, but he didn't like the feeling and he stood. "I have lots to do today, so I'll be on my way." He raised his hand in a half wave and made his way to the door. As he closed it, he caught a glimpse of surprise on her face. He suspected it matched his own surprise.

Sitting in Devon's backyard, Ashley had tried to find a moment to apologize for her sharp retort when she'd last seen him. She owed him that. She'd hurt him. He'd stayed away for a few days, and though she knew part of his absence meant he was working, she'd also noticed his car in and out of his driveway a couple of times. She hadn't deciphered why she'd spoken as she had to him, although she suspected the reason. Devon had gotten into her bloodstream, and he had almost become the air she breathed.

The pastor's message the Sunday Devon had attended hung in her thoughts. She'd allowed her worries to cover the hope she'd felt that day. Even the choir's anthem had become her prayer. *I need Thee, oh, I need Thee.* Yet she didn't hear if the Lord spoke to her or not. Instead, she listened to her own negativity.

But Devon had called the evening of her appointment to see about her cast. When she heard his voice, her heart sang, and she told him the good news. She had a walking cast, and though she still had to be careful and keep the crutches handy, she had taken her first careful step, balancing her body against the weight of her left leg.

Joey's giggle followed Kaylee's, and Ashley lifted her head from her musing to see what was funny. A butterfly had rested on a flower Kaylee had picked from the garden to fill a small vase Devon had given her. With their exuberance, it flitted away.

Freedom. What would it be like to fly away from danger at will? To sense when to stay and when to go? She thought she had that sense, that wisdom, but she'd been wrong. Since meeting Devon, she could not measure her own judgment. What made her feel whole tore her apart. It was senseless.

The screen door banged, and she turned, seeing Devon come from the house carrying a plate of burgers covered in plastic wrap. He checked the grill and set the plate on the table before heading her way. "Need a refill?"

She eyed her iced tea and shook her head. "I'm fine." No, the tea was fine. She was a mess.

"Good." He slipped into the nearby chair. "We haven't really had private time to talk." He made a subtle motion toward the children. "I'm letting things slide for now. I want to give Gina time to cool down and think about the offer. I hope she'll reconsider."

His positive attitude made her envy him. "You still think she'll come around."

He gave her a one-shoulder shrug. "Notice I said hope." He leaned closer. "Remember the Bible verse that Sunday? *Trust in the Lord with all your heart and lean not on your own understanding.* I memorized it." He pressed his shoulders against the canvas chair back. "Sometimes I wonder how I've gotten by without those words."

She lowered her eyes as shame knotted in her chest. She'd been the strong Christian. Devon hadn't been as much. So what happened? She forced her head upward. "I'm glad the message gave you hope...and trust." Then a confession spiraled to her throat. "I wish I could cling to those words as well as you do."

A look of surprise registered on his face, then faded as quickly. "Why can't it, Ashley?"

"I wish I knew. I take one negative moment in my life and use it as my life pattern." Her example surged through her. "It's almost as if I see it as my goal rather than a lesson to help my life be better." She pressed her hand to her chest, fearing her heart would break through. "I don't know why I'm telling you this."

"Because I want to know about you. Can't you see that? Friends share their hearts. You have a difficult time doing that."

"I wasn't allowed to when I was growing up. I kept my hurts and comments to myself. It was safer."

His expression darkened. "Is this about your mother?" He shook his head. "I probably shouldn't have asked, but I heard a little of what you and Neely talked about the last time I was there."

"I felt badly about that." She leaned closer and touched his hand, knowing she had to be open. "I guessed you wanted to know more, and I couldn't talk about it then. I feel guilty that I have negative feelings about my mother, and I took it out on you." Her throat tightened with emotion as unwanted tears blurred her vision. "I'm sorry. I am so very sorry."

His hands wrapped around hers. "I knew you were upset. I wasn't sure why, and I thought it was because of me. I thought I'd done something to anger you. I worry about being presumptuous. I've told you that." His fingers brushed the top of her hand, soothing her mind.

"Devon, do you see that you're holding something, too? You spent your life since marriage believing you couldn't meet Gina's needs, and it wasn't you at all."

His fingers weaved through hers. "I guess we're both dealing with baggage we don't need anymore."

She pressed her free hand over his. "You're right. Let's work on that."

For the first time that day, they smiled.

He glanced toward the barbecue. "I'd better get those burgers cooked before we hear complaints from the flower children."

She turned her head and laughed again. Joey and Kaylee had used the flowers they'd picked to decorate their hair. They reminded her of the flower children she'd seen in photos from the seventies.

Joey ran toward her, his arms opened and flailing up and down. "I'm a butterfly, Mama."

"You are. You're my butterfly." And one day she prayed she could be one, too. Free of her fears. Her gaze drifted to Devon, the kind of man any woman could love.

Chapter Eleven

Devon ascended the stairs behind Ashley, making sure she didn't have a problem with her new walking cast. A weight had lifted from him today when they'd talked about important things that opened doors of understanding.

After they'd eaten, Joey played with Kaylee, and then he fell asleep on the floor. When nine o'clock showed on the clock, Devon laid him on the guest bed while Kaylee readied herself for sleep. His custom of reading to her before bedtime was waylaid by Ashley's presence. Kaylee hadn't mentioned it, but his own guilt did. He would read twice as much the next time she stayed with him.

When Ashley reached the top of the stairs, she grasped the handrail and faced him. "Your home is lovely. I see a piece of you in every room. I'd thought I might see more of..." She frowned. "I should keep my mouth shut."

"You mean Gina, and you don't have to avoid any comments." He'd reached her and slid his arm around her back. "She didn't have a lot of interest in decorating. I was surprised. I asked her opinion, and she said yes to most everything I suggested." He shook his head, remembering what he'd thought back then. "She seemed so agreeable and willing to cooperate. I was thrilled, but obviously I was naive. I think that was part of her illness showing up in our lives that early."

"Depression causes those reactions, I've heard."

"This way." He guided her down the hall to the sitting room off his bedroom where the door opened to the second-floor balcony. "Here's your chair and the view." He motioned to the full sky above, now dissipating to lavender and deep red. "It'll be ten soon. That's when they start."

"Really special. And I love the sitting room. My bedroom is small compared to this one."

"The others are smaller." He stood behind her and rested his hands on her shoulders. "I'm going to check on the kids one more time, and then I'll run down and bring us up a treat."

She tilted her head around. "Take your time. I'm enjoying the warm breeze and the sunset."

He headed downstairs, reviewing the day they'd had. A good day. The kids were great and got along well. The talk with Ashley had eased the tension between them, and he'd learned something new. He'd allowed a warped view of himself to influence his relationship with her. Now having grasped his new perspective, he would work to help Ashley see that her mother's behavior didn't affect who she was. He hoped that was all that held her back.

In the kitchen, he poured drinks and scooped up portions of the peach cobbler Ashley had brought to the picnic, then headed up the stairs. By the time he'd stepped onto the balcony, the inky sky displayed only a sliver of moon, adding to the darkness.

Ashley looked over her shoulder. "Good night for fireworks."

His mind flashed. A good night for many things. "It is." He handed her the dessert and set her drink on the table beside her. When he settled in the chair, he leaned back and drew in the fresh air, cooler now that the sun had set.

Though he would enjoy the fireworks, his concentration stayed more on Ashley so close beside him, the fragrance of flowers wrapped around him. Her lotion. He'd smelled it before, and he'd seen her use it on her hands.

He picked up the cobbler as perfect as Ashley. Sweet, tender. He chuckled and realized she'd heard him. "You can do about anything, even bake the best peach cobbler I've ever had."

"Thank you, but you should know I can't do everything."

Her gaze captured his, and he understood too well what she meant. She couldn't make a decision, one that he longed for her to make.

He slipped his hand over hers and brushed the back with his palm.

Instead of pulling away, Ashley rotated her hand and weaved her fingers through his. As she squeezed, the first sizzle of fireworks soared into the sky, golden squiggles that buzzed away with another burst like an orange chrysanthemum.

Another followed, and she released his fingers, shifted forward and managed to stand, her fingers grasping the balcony railing.

Devon rose and stood beside her, slipping his arm around her back as she leaned into him. It was as if they'd never talked about remaining friends only. Tonight a different essence filled the night and his heart. His hope warmed him. Words clung to his lips. Things he longed to say but feared her rejection.

Wisdom told him to keep his declaration inside. Instead, he refocused on the colorful display filling the sky while his senses lavished in Ashley's softness at his side, her tender touch.

"What a night." She turned to him, their lips so close he could taste the sweetness.

Willing determination, he nodded. "Special."

She dragged in a deep breath. "Very."

The single word meant so much to him. The sound enveloped his being. Very. He drew her closer, and she yielded as the sky burst into color, spinning, soaring, blossoming like flowers. His heart stood still, and when he gazed at her, she tilted her face upward, offering her lips. He met them, his pulse soaring. Her lips touched his, gentle yet firm, alive and sweet. Her arms raised around his neck, and his hopes swelled and spiraled like the colors in the sky.

They turned together at the final blast when the dark sky turned into a prism of light and color, shapes and motion, the same sensations he'd experienced with the kiss.

As the colors faded and drifted to the ground, leaving hazy smoke in the sky, he guided Ashley into the chair and settled beside her, wanting to talk but not knowing what to say that wouldn't turn her "very" response into leaden haze.

"It's late. I should go." Her voice seemed a whisper.

Though he had to work tomorrow, he hated the night to end. "Now? You sure?"

"Please."

Her tone answered his question. Tonight was not the moment for making sense of what they'd just shared. He'd waited this long while his feelings grew. He could wait a little longer.

If she were a slammer, Ashley would have banged the kitchen cabinet door closed when she arrived home from Devon's. He'd been attentive as always, carrying Joey up to his guest room and tucking him into bed before helping her up the stairs to view the fireworks. When they had returned to the first floor, he'd promised to bring back her dishes from the picnic tomorrow.

Tomorrow. How could she face him in the daylight, with the moon and stars no longer in the sky? Face him after the glorious colors bursting and flitting through the air now that reality had set in.

How could she face herself? She'd wanted the kiss as badly as he did. Denying her feelings compared to swallowing a boulder. Impossible. Her thoughts centered around Devon. His image hung in her mind no matter what she did. She smiled thinking of his witty comments or his thoughtful ways. He'd enveloped her life.

But in the light of day, every sound of a siren or every newscast of a fire or another tragedy, caused bile to rise in her throat. Her stomach knotted into a tangle of fear and foreshadowing. One day someone would come to her door to bear the horrible news that her husband had been killed while on duty. He'd died to save others' lives.

Too real. Too horrifying. She'd experienced that once. Three years had passed since the doorbell had rung and the uniformed men appeared on her porch. Never again. The uniforms would be different, but the message would be the same. Died in the line of duty to protect, to save, to aid. Who would protect her then? Who would save her next time? She didn't have the strength to live through it again.

She sank onto a kitchen chair and buried her face in her hands, tears wetting her fingers, her center barraged with hopes and dreams slamming into the darker images. *Lord, why? Why does this kind, loving, caring man have a career that screamed death and loss? Why can't I overcome my fears and worries?*

Her thoughts shriveled as silence filled her mind. From somewhere deep, words flowed into her thoughts like a soft voice, so hushed she could barely make out the sounds. *Trust in the Lord—He is your help and shield.*

She ran her knuckles across her damp eyes and inched her head upward, searching for the source of the voice, yet she knew the search would be fruitless. God's Word had spoken a reminder of her faith. Trust in the Lord and lean not on her own understanding.

Trust. The word that caught in her throat and muddied her mind.

"Lord, help me trust You." Her voice broke the silence of her kitchen. She'd sometimes questioned the depth of her faith. Tonight offered another example of why she asked the question. A Christian had to lay her burdens at Jesus' feet and walk away, not cling to them as if they were precious gifts.

She rose and slid the chair beneath the table, swallowed a drink of water from the glass she'd filled and poured the rest into the sink. She turned off the light and made her way up the stairs to her bedroom. With each step, she offered a whispered prayer. "I lay my burdens at Your feet and trust in You, Lord."

As Devon listened to Kaylee singing to herself from the living room, he sat in the kitchen staring at the clock. He'd returned Ashley's dishes from the picnic the next day as he'd promised, but he'd only set them on the counter and made an excuse to leave.

He cared more than he could say, but he was tired of the ups and downs with Ashley. Her mind had been dented by something in her past—her mother, her last romantic experience or a deep love for her deceased husband that she couldn't move past. Something. If she cared enough she would tell him, screamed in his mind. He'd admitted the flaw he thought had caused his failed marriage. Now he'd learned the truth. Though his work schedule didn't help the situation, the greatest issue now eased his mind. Gina had an illness she couldn't control, one that would never be cured.

Since he'd opened up, why couldn't Ashley tell him what bothered her? If she did, they could make it right, but if she clung to the problem, it would fester like a wound until any hope for a relationship would be lost. His heart grew heavy with the idea.

His earlier worry vanished when after a short time Joey and Kaylee melded into an easy relationship. No more comments about age or gender. They'd become like brother and sister. His pulse clipped as the image settled in his mind.

Since the touchy encounter with Ashley, he'd bitten off his nose to spite his face, as the old saying went. He missed Joey, and Kaylee asked more than once why they hadn't visited Ashley and Joey. He rose and ambled to the living room, observing Kaylee from the doorway. She lay on the sofa, a book propped open on her tummy, but her mind seemed to be somewhere else since her eyes were closed and she sang a song about wishing on a star. He recognized it from one of the CDs she enjoyed.

"You sing pretty." He moved closer and sat on the edge of the sofa near her feet. He reached out to tickle them, and she jerked them up.

She grinned, trying to tuck her feet beneath the cushion he was sitting on.

Devon loved hearing her laugh. "That song's from a movie."

She nodded. *"Pinocchio."* She clamped two fingers on her nose and stretched. "If he lied, his nose got longer and longer."

"You'll never have a long nose, will you?" He hoped she'd say she never lied.

Her expression became thoughtful. "I don't want a long nose."

That didn't answer his question, but he managed to chuckle. "I think you're a little bored. Should I read to you?" He drew his back straighter. "Better yet, how about you take a turn first?" He motioned toward her stack of books on the table.

"Okay, but you read to me." She slid the books around, pulled out one and handed it to him.

"Don't you like to read out loud?" He eyed the book and recognized it as one he'd read her often. "I thought your aunt Renee and your mom had you read aloud."

She shrugged. "Aunt Renee helps me."

His chest tightened seeing the expression on her face. "Not your mom?"

She lowered her head, evading his eyes. "She's…"

Her hand shifted upward as if touching her nose, and he knew what bothered her. "You can tell me, Kaylee. Remember. I won't ever make you do something you don't want to do."

Her head shot upward, her gaze latching on to his. "But I want to, Daddy."

"You want to tell me? That's good."

"No." She shook her head as she responded. "Yes, I want to tell you, but what I really want is to live with you."

His heart careened in his chest. This wasn't what he'd expected, and though he loved hearing her say it, he knew the change would result in a confrontation.

"I'd love to have you here." He dropped the book beside him and wrapped her in his arms. "But why do you want to leave your aunt Renee's? What's happened?"

Her gaze shifted again. "Mom's…" She sent him a plaintive look. "Mommy's in the hospital again, and I don't know when she'll get out."

His limbs grew numb, frozen in time. Kaylee cuddled in his protective arms and needed his response. Words weighted his mind. What to say? What to do? He listened, and the answer came. "I'll talk to your aunt Renee when she's home from work. Is that what you'd like?"

"She'll be mad at me." Her eyes locked with his again.

"All you did was tell me the truth." He lifted his hand and touched the end of her nose with his index finger. "Your nose is the same size it was this morning."

His comment brought a grin to her face. "Cuz I didn't fib."

"Right. You told me what bothered you, and it needed saying."

Her eyes filled with tears. "I love you, Daddy."

"I love you, sweetheart." He scooted her onto his lap and wrapped her in his arms. "You know I have to work long hours. We'll have to find a place for you to stay when I'm on duty."

"With Ashley. I can stay there." She lifted her head from his shoulder. "I wish we would go visit Ashley now like we always do."

"How about…" His heartbeat escalated as it had been doing lately when he thought of Ashley. He longed to talk with her, and now Kaylee's request gave him impetus. Having her live with him had been his dream, a complicated situation, but what he'd always wanted. Now it could come true, but he needed help and he didn't think Ashley would be the answer. Not the way things sat with them.

Kaylee's head cocked, her eyes searching his. "How about what, Daddy?"

Needing time to think, he tossed around options. "How about we go after dinner?"

"How about now, and we could order a pizza for all of us?" She gave him a Cheshire cat grin.

His time to think crumbled. To Kaylee, his need to think would be beyond her comprehension. And even worse, he had no idea how Ashley would react when he arrived at her door. Calling was out of the question. The only way was face-to-face.

He grasped her cheeks in his hands and kissed Kaylee's forehead. "I suppose we could take a walk over there, but don't be disappointed if she...she already has dinner planned." Or she doesn't want to see your dad. That's more likely. His shoulders drooped.

Kaylee swung her legs to the floor and bounced up, unaware of his reticence. "Let's go." The book she'd selected fell to the floor as she rose. She lay it back on the vacated cushion before she skipped toward the front door, beckoning him to come.

Her eagerness caught in his chest. Allowing his confusion to monitor what he'd wanted to do all along didn't work for him or Kaylee. If he were a betting man, he'd wager

Ashley's kiss the other night meant exactly what he felt. She cared for him. Cared deeply. But they both had tiptoed around, clinging to past issues, and no progress would ever be made that way.

While Kaylee stood in the open front door, he buried his thoughts and rose from the sofa, longing to see Ashley but how they were together weeks ago, before their kisses put a twisted spin on their relationship. He strode to the door and followed Kaylee outside. As she skipped along, singing the wishing-on-a-star song, he added his own wish for a smoother road for Ashley and him. If their relationship was to be nothing, he needed to know.

He couldn't bear the thought.

Chapter Twelve

"Devon."

Joey's piping voice startled Ashley. She hit the footrest handle and lowered her legs as the doorbell rang. She eyed the door, waiting for it to open.

Instead, she heard his knock.

Joey flattened his face against the front window, cupping his eyes from the sun, and let out a yell. "Hi, Kaylee."

The excitement in his voice had to penetrate the window, but Devon seemed determined that she answer the door. Though she understood, it broke her heart. Why did they get themselves tangled in all the foolishness? She knew the answer before it left her mouth.

Ashley opened the door. Kaylee entered first, and she greeted her with a hug. Then she opened the door wider. "Devon." Regret she'd been unable to hide sounded in her voice. "It's nice to see you."

Joey reached toward him, his arms as wide as his grin.

Devon scooped him into the air and nuzzled his face into his neck and blew.

Joey squirmed and giggled, and when he stopped, Joey didn't. "More tickle."

But Devon's gaze shifted to Kaylee. Instead of more tickles for Joey, he ruffled the boy's hair and swung him to the floor, then drew Kaylee closer and tickled her neck with his fingers.

That seemed all she needed. She giggled, too, and darted away from him as she grabbed Joey's hand. Together, they bounded across the room to the toy box and Devon stood facing her. "Kaylee kept asking to come over and—"

"I meant what I said." Her stomach constricted as she motioned toward the easy chair. "It's nice to see you." Her eyes sought his. "I miss you."

He stood as if transfixed. "I miss you, too."

As if the words were an anchor, their eyes locked, and wholeness buoyed her spirit, a wholeness she'd lost with Adam's death, and though the sensation warmed her, an uneasy feeling remained.

She managed to step aside without leaping into his arms, and Devon followed her invitation, settling into the easy chair. Returning to the recliner, she sank into the cushion and lifted the footrest.

"How's the leg?" The question came casually though it seemed mundane when compared with the many issues that often made the air seem heavy.

"I'm doing okay except for the stairs, especially when I have to carry something, but I'm becoming a pro." She managed a grin and he smiled back, although she still noted the strain in his face.

"I have so much to tell you, but…"

She waited, her attention hanging on his unfinished sentence. "But?"

He shook his head. "I don't know where to begin."

She froze in place, icy thoughts slipping

into her mind. Was this goodbye? Though she'd seen it as an answer to her fears, the possibility sank her into an abyss. "Start anywhere, Devon. Just tell me."

"Two things."

His abrupt response unsettled her. Two things? She swallowed. "The first?"

His head eased upward and his eyes captured hers. "I'll go with the easiest one." His gaze shot to Kaylee.

She followed his lead and saw Kaylee and Joey seemingly preoccupied with a jigsaw puzzle. Her focus returned to Devon.

"Kaylee asked to live with me today."

Her heart stopped as the idea reveled in her mind. "Really? She asked?"

He nodded. "Seems her mother's back in the hospital, and she said she wasn't sure when she'll get out." He lifted his shoulders and let them drop. "I have to get to the bottom of this with Renee. I'll call her tonight when she's home from work."

Ashley let the vision weave through her mind. Kaylee would add a complication to his work schedule, and her first reaction was to volunteer to help him. Kaylee could stay with her on the nights Devon worked. The guest room was perfect. But they had something else to discuss, according to Devon, and where would that leave them? Goodbye? Hello? Confusion thumped in her brain. No response was possible until she heard what he had to say.

"You'll have a clearer picture once you talk to her, but I wonder what caused Gina to go back so soon? I suppose that's the question."

"She's ill. We talked about it the other day. Gina's struggled with depression even before I realized it. I've come to face that, but now I realize how the pattern has continued. Her illness seems to be more severe. It's heartbreaking for Kaylee to live through it day in and out at Renee's. It's not a life for a child."

"It's not." Words seemed empty. Nothing she could say now could help since their relationship was up in the air. She studied his face, wanting to encourage him to tell her the second thing on his mind.

A stream of air left his lungs and he leaned back against the chair cushion. "That's number one." He closed his eyes and sat in silence.

Her nerves grew taut in the stillness. She

wanted to scream. Instead, she released her own pent-up breath and prayed.

When he opened his eyes, his face had relaxed. "The next thing is so confusing for both of us. We're struggling with…"

She held her breath.

"With us. I guess that's how to put it. With our relationship." He lifted his eyes to hers. "You know what I'm talking about."

She nodded. "We both have issues, I guess."

Devon leaned forward, resting his elbows on his knees, his hands folded. Before he spoke, his gaze shifted to Kaylee again and then back to her. "Mine have become less now that I realized maybe I'm not the rotten husband I feared I was. The thing I can't change is my work schedule. It's part of the job I do."

"I don't see that as a problem for anyone except Kaylee's care." She only mouthed the child's name not to draw the little girl's attention to their conversation on the other side of the room.

He gave his head a bounce as if accepting her comment. "But we still have things to talk about." He pulled his back straight. "I need to understand what bothers you, Ashley. I need the truth. Could we have a cola or coffee? Anything." He used his head to direct her toward the dining room.

She understood and lowered the footrest, then used the chair arm to hoist herself upward on her one unencumbered leg. She turned and hobbled through the archway.

Devon followed and moved past her to pull out a chair. "Sit. I'll get us something. What do you want?"

"Water with ice is fine for me."

He didn't respond but scooted past her and vanished into the kitchen.

She maneuvered her leg beneath the table and shifted around, her gaze on Devon in the kitchen making himself at home. She loved seeing him comfortable there.

In a moment, he returned and set the water in front of her. She took a sip, not realizing how worry had dried her throat. When she set down the glass, she turned her attention to Devon. "Tell me what you want to know."

He stared at her a moment, a look of surprise softening to concern. "Just tell me if I'm right, okay?"

His suggestion seemed more convoluted, but she nodded in agreement.

"You care about me." He lifted his gaze to hers. "More than care."

His questioning eyes filled her heart. She couldn't lie to him, though she wished she could. "Yes, I care very much."

"You're worried about whether I can stick with a relationship long term. Afraid I'll walk away from you in bad times."

"Absolutely not, Devon. You were faithful to Gina, and I think you'd still be married to her if she'd stuck with you. It was her failure not yours."

His eyes glazed as if trying to comprehend what she'd said. "Then it's not me."

"It's not you, Devon. It's..."

"Adam. You're still in love with him and can't let go."

A rattled sigh fluttered from her chest. "No. It's not Adam. Yes, I love him, but I have let him go not only for my sake but for Joey's." She shook her head. "It's my head, Devon. It's all in my head and my weak faith."

He drew back, a look of surprise bursting on his face. "You don't have weak faith. How can you say that? I've watched you—"

Her cell phone jangled, and Devon halted, his gaze on the phone.

"Devon, I—"

"Answer it." He waved his hand toward it. "We've waited this long."

She eyed Neely's name on the caller ID. The interruption gave them a short detour. She'd been ready to talk if only to quiet Devon's fears, but their talk needed time.

The cell rang a third time. She pulled her gaze away from Devon and answered.

"Paula just called to tell us Aunt Florence died."

Ashley closed her eyes. "We should have gone to visit and not listened to Paula. Now I feel guilty."

"Don't feel guilty, Ash. We offered and she discouraged us, but now it's different. Paula needs our support. I was surprised at how broken up she was."

"I suppose it's regret." Ashley's memory took her back to the difficult years with her mother. "She's like us, Neely, wishing she and her mother had gotten along better. I wonder if she knows why her mother and Mom were both so closed up, so unwilling to say something nice."

"She's probably in the same situation we are. Mom's gone and now Aunt Florence. We may never know."

Ashley rubbed her temple, her question still niggling her thoughts until Neely's question broke her musing.

"We should go now, don't you think?"

Ashley eyed her cast. "We need to. With no siblings, we're about as close to a sister as Paula will ever have." Joey's voice drifted in from the living room. "I wonder if Dad could watch Joey for me."

"Take him with us. I'm sure Dad will come up for the funeral anyway."

"I hate to drag him along, but I suppose I will."

"Should we leave tonight? We can get there in time to help with the details. It's about a three-hour drive. Maybe a little longer."

Ashley's gaze shifted toward Devon. The call had interrupted their talk, and now… "I'll get ready. Give me an hour, okay?"

Neely agreed, and when Ashley ended the call, a hollow feeling crept through her. She lifted her gaze to Devon. "My aunt died, and we're going to leave tonight. Paula has no one, and I know she needs support. She lives near Roscommon."

"Kaylee and I were talking about ordering pizza for dinner. I'll take Joey for you tonight and tomorrow, but I'll be back to work the following day so maybe you could work something else out for that."

"Are you sure, Devon? I hate dumping on you again."

"Dumping? I love time with Joey, and Kaylee's great with him now." He gave her a silly look. "How about your dad for Saturday?"

"That will probably be the funeral. Dad could bring Joey with him. That won't be a problem." A knot formed in her chest. "You're sure?"

"Positive." He rose and slid his chair back. "What can I do to get Joey ready to go?"

"You're a lifesaver, Devon." As the words left her mouth, she realized he really was, and that was their major problem. As she made her way off the chair, the irony caught in her throat. "I owe you one, Devon." She slipped her arm around his waist. "I owe you two."

He lifted his index finger and touched her lower lip, and her heart sang.

Devon grinned. "Maybe three or four."

She understood, and despite her resistance, she loved his affection.

The children tucked into their beds, Devon poured a glass of cola and sat beside the phone. He had to call Renee before the reasonable time to make a call passed him by. Eight-thirty wasn't too late. He grasped the receiver and hit the phone number. He hoped Renee would answer and not her husband. Dwight had a tendency to block calls to Renee and wanted to deal with the issue himself. This problem needed Renee's cooperation.

His palm grew sweaty as he waited for someone to answer, and when he heard Renee's voice, a flash of relief spurred him forward. "We need to discuss Kaylee's well-being."

"Well-being? What are you talking about?"

"Gina's in the hospital again, and Kaylee is disturbed. She asked to live with me, and I think that's the best solution we have, Renee. She needs to have at least one parent."

"Do you think I don't care about her well-being, Devon. I've nearly raised your daughter."

"I'm not doubting your ability." He sucked in air. "But you just said the key word. Kaylee is my daughter."

"I don't believe she asked to live with you, Devon. I think you've put words—"

"Stop right there, Renee. I did not coach or even suggest that possibility to her. We were looking at books and I suggested she read one to me. I know you've been working with her on sounding out words. That's when she told me about her mother's hospitalization."

Renee's sigh rattled from the phone. "I asked her to avoid that subject, and I—"

"And I asked you to stop telling her to lie. She—"

"Devon, I said 'avoid' not 'lie.' I've never asked her to lie."

The conversation would go nowhere if they got hung up on that issue. He tried to refocus. "I've never asked Gina to give up custody. Kaylee has always lived with her since my work has always been a scheduling problem. I appreciate that you've worked with me on this, but since Gina is in the hospital more than she's home, the arrangement is senseless. I want to spend quality time with my daughter, and I think it's time she moved here with me."

"I think not. Anyway, the decision is her mother's, and until you get that, you'll have to accept the present arrangements."

A chill rolled down his arms as icy thoughts coursed through his brain. Dealing with Renee seemed useless, and his only hope was to get a lawyer behind him, but he didn't want to drag Kaylee into court to state her decision. He couldn't hurt her like that. His mind spun as it thawed, and a new argument slipped inside. "Let's not argue over this, Renee. We both want what's best for Kaylee. She asked to stay here, and I'm willing to make it temporary until Gina is home again. When that happens I'll discuss the situation with her."

"But you still have your work schedule. What's your plan?"

He closed his eyes, hoping to hide the anger growing in his voice. "You work, Renee. What's your plan? I don't question Kaylee's care while you're working. I trust you love her enough to find good people to watch her. I don't expect you to question me. I'll make arrangements for good care for her just as I assume you do. Do you understand?"

The line fell silent. He dragged in a breath wondering what new argument she would come up with, and then he heard her clear her throat.

"Can I call you tomorrow, Devon? After I give this some thought."

"What is there to think about? I'm asking for temporary custody of my daughter. That's all. She can visit you when she wants, and you're welcome to visit here. I know she's been part of your life for the past three years."

"Closer to four years now."

He ignored her comment. "What do you say?"

Silence pulsed over the line. "Can I talk with her?"

"She's in bed sleeping. It's going on nine." A stream of air whispered in his ear.

"When do you want to make the change?"

The question startled him. He'd anticipated a bigger battle. Grateful, he considered the situation with Ashley gone and made his decision. "I'll bring her home on Saturday and you can have the weekend together. Monday I'll come by my usual time, and I can pack up her things—what she'll need here—or if you and Kaylee want to do that over the weekend that's fine."

"We'll pack her things. No need for you to get involved with that. She'll be ready on Monday."

"Thanks, Renee." Another issue struck him. "Will you tell Gina or should I?"

"Gina's in no condition right now to deal with anything. I'll talk to her when the time is right. Then the situation is up to you."

Her admission startled him. "What's wrong with her this time?"

The silence stretched.

"Renee, what is it?"

Another blast of air, then he heard her voice. "She tried to kill herself, Devon. Kaylee doesn't know this, so be careful what you say."

Gina? He pictured her years earlier when he'd fallen in love. She always had a side of her he couldn't understand—those quiet moods of withdrawal. Later he recognized it as depression. She took medication sometimes, but to be so desperate to want to kill herself? He couldn't grasp the concept. "I'm startled, Renee, as you can guess."

"I'm sorry, Devon. I've tried to protect you from that."

Something hedged in her words. "You mean, she's done this before?"

"Yes. It's not the first."

Terror rankled him. Could she hurt Kaylee? Perhaps Gina had feared what she might do, and that was why she wanted to be around people. Could that have been why she'd left their marriage? And if so, did the fear remain? He couldn't take the chance. He needed to obtain full custody of his beautiful daughter before something happened, something he would regret forever.

"Thanks for being honest. I'll bring her to you Saturday and pick her up on Monday as we planned. You do what you think's right with Gina. I'll leave that in your hands."

She said goodbye and he hung up, his mind tangled in knots of concern and grief. How could a lovely woman like Gina want to destroy her life, destroy her daughter's opportunity to grow up with a mother's love? He closed his eyes, unable to imagine Gina's plight.

Ashley slipped off her shoes and curled her good leg beneath her on the sofa. Her gaze shifted past the sterile decor to her cousin seated in a wingback chair closest to the telephone. Paula had aged since they'd seen each other, but then so had she. But age didn't diminish Paula's good looks. Her long wavy hair matched the color of her caramel eyes. If she smiled, she would be striking.

Ashley scanned the walls, lacking paintings or wall hangings—beige walls with windows the only item to break the muted scene, but even then the shades had been pulled, beige shades beside beige draperies. *Sterile* seemed the perfect word.

Paula leaned back her slippered feet resting on an ottoman that matched the chair. "Thanks for coming so fast and helping with the decisions. I dreaded handling it all alone."

Neely pulled her shoulder from the edge of the archway, a coffee mug in her hand. "We were glad to come. I remember too well what it was like when Mother died."

Paula averted her gaze. "I'm sorry I didn't come for the visitation or the funeral. I'm not even sure Mother let me know."

Ashley jumped at the opportunity to address their mother's past. "Our mothers had a lot in common. I don't know if you realize that."

"It makes sense." Paula lifted her gaze, but didn't say more.

"They were sisters." Neely's injection hung with question.

Paula wiggled deeper into the cushion. "Sisters and so much more from what Mother told me before she died. I suppose that's why I'm sorry for the way I reacted to her coldness."

"We don't know what happened." Ashley leaned closer, her arms crossed, resting on her knees. "Is this something you just learned?"

Paula nodded. "You mean, your mother never talked about their uncle?"

Ashley dashed a look toward Neely, who shrugged. "We didn't know she had an uncle."

"It would have been better if they hadn't." She lowered her head and stared at the carpet. "It cleared up the questions I had for so long, but it opened other doors I'll never have answers for."

Gooseflesh rose on Ashley's arms. "What happened? Can you tell us about it?"

"Maybe we'll understand our mom better, that is, if you feel like talking." Neely plopped into a matching chair across from Paula.

Tension grew on Paula's face. "Our mothers' uncle—their dad's brother—lived with them, and when their dad died, he tried to come on to their mother but she put him in his place. At least this is what my mother noticed happening." She shook her head. "I don't know why she didn't ask him to move, but I think it had to do with money. He paid room and board, and Dad's illness ate up a lot of their savings."

Trying to understand how this affected her mother, Ashley caught Neely's eyes and gave a subtle shrug.

Neely shrugged back. "But what does that have to do with our mothers?"

Paula bit her lip. "My mother didn't say much about your mom, but what she said about herself led me to believe it affected yours, too."

"What affected them?" Ashley wished she'd stop hemming and tell them.

"I think their uncle didn't give up. When your mother ran off and married your dad, the uncle began to bother my mother. I suspect he went right down the line—their mother first, then your mother, and then mine, trying to satiate his lust."

Ashley heard Neely gasp. She'd swallowed her reaction, wishing Paula was wrong.

Paula gave a nod, acknowledging Neely's startled reaction. "It's even worse. He'd grab at my mother, and when she rejected him, as your mother must have done, he started telling her she was ugly and not worth a nickle. He'd tell her if she wanted to know a man, he was her only bet."

The hairs prickled on Ashley's arms. "You think he did the same to our mother?"

"I'm quite sure. Mom said that Aunt Marion got more and more withdrawn, and at night she'd barricade her door. Mother knew it because one time she wanted to talk with her, and she had a chair propped under the doorknob and had to move it. All she said was she felt safer."

"That's horrible." Ashley didn't want to believe what she was hearing. "Did he hurt Aunt Florence?" What she wanted to know was did he hurt her mother?

"Mom didn't go into details, but it's possible. She always seemed a little cold to my dad, and she was very critical of everyone.

Very suspicious. When I wanted to date, she forbade it. She told me men were no good, except they worked and paid the bills. I looked at my kind father, and it made me sick. I moved away as soon as I had a job and a place to stay."

Ashley glanced at Neely, recalling how she'd moved to Chicago right after college, and marriage hadn't been on her mind until she came back home and Jon stepped into her life. "Thanks for telling us, Paula."

Neely added her thanks. "I think we can better understand Mom's hard exterior. We wanted our mother to be like our friends' moms were. She didn't have it in her, but if I grew up dodging a demeaning relative whose only thought was to use me for his purposes, I might have been like Mom."

Ashley rose and settled on the arm of Paula's chair, slipping her arm around her shoulders. "You've cleared up so much. Our dad knows this, I think, but he'd never explained what was wrong. He just accepted it."

Paula rested her head on Ashley's shoulder. "Maybe he didn't know the details, but if he did, he wouldn't say anything because he's a good man. I always liked your dad."

"Then you have to come and visit us, Paula. Once you get things settled here, please come. Neely's getting married in a few weeks and Dad will have a free room and I have a guest room at my house. We'd love you to come. We're as close as you'll ever get to sisters."

"We'd love it." Neely rose and walked to her side.

Tears filled Paula's eyes. "Thanks so much for the invitation. I've never had a brother or a sister. Two sisters sound amazing."

"You can stay as long as you want, Paula. I know you've had a difficult life, and we don't expect you to spill it out for us." Ashley knew from her mother that Paula had had a rough past. Her mother let them know that. "Having you nearby would be special."

"I don't deserve this, but I thank you so much." Paula looked from one to the other. "Maybe one day I can talk about my rotten life, but for now, it's wonderful having you here to help me get through the funeral."

"Sisters." Ashley and Neely gave her a high five.

Paula flexed her hand and leaned in to meet theirs. It was the first time they'd seen her smile since they'd arrived.

Chapter Thirteen

Though surrounded by firefighters he considered friends, Devon felt lonely as he finished his last report. This time the emptiness wasn't from missing Kaylee. Instead, he was preoccupied with thoughts of Ashley. She'd been gone since Friday and arrived home last night. So much had happened since they'd talked, and his news wasn't meant for a phone call. He wanted to see her reaction and hear what she had to say.

He put his last report on the captain's desk, slipped out of his gear and put on street clothes. As he stepped into the hallway, Clint sidled up to him, as always with a coy smile on his face.

"Picking up that little girl of yours today?" Clint was the one man he talked to about everything. Though not much older than he, Clint had a wise head on his shoulders.

"Today's the day. I know she's excited. I talked with her last night when I had a minute and she was packed and ready to go."

"It'll be different for you, but I know from the smile on your face this change is what you've waited for." Clint rested his hand on Devon's shoulder. "But it won't be easy, either. You'll be torn when she's ill and you can't be there. I hope you have family or someone you trust to care for her."

Devon's stomach did a yo-yo bounce. "Ashley volunteered to let her stay with her and Joey. I'll pay her, and I know Kaylee's in good hands. In an emergency, I have my parents."

"Ashley's a good lady." Clint tilted his head, his gaze probing Devon's. "Nothing happening between you two yet?" His expression carried a hint of concern. "You're not going to let this woman slip through your fingers, are you?"

Devon glanced at his hand, thinking of

Ashley's dark hair grazing his fingers. "I'm working on it. She's a slow mover, and we almost got down to basics when a call interrupted our talk." He shrugged. "Her aunt died, and she had to go out of town that night."

"Bad timing."

"She's home, and I'm hoping today we can finish the conversation. You'll know the result when you see me on Wednesday. You have a knack for reading my face."

Clint slapped his back. "It's easy to read, pal. You haven't learned the art of masking your feelings."

He grinned, facing that skill had failed him. He stuck out his hand and shook Clint's. "Enjoy your days off, buddy. I hope to do the same."

Clint double clasped his fingers. "I'll pray that it's a good one for you…all the way around."

The comment left Devon no question. Having custody of Kaylee and resolving the relationship with Ashley was almost more than one day could hold, but he couldn't wait.

When he rolled into Renee's driveway,

Kaylee's nose was pressed to the window. She bounded backward as if connected to a rubber sling and shot out the front door. He hurried from the car to greet her, and while she toted a box to his trunk, he grasped the two pieces of luggage Renee had set on the porch.

Kaylee leaned the box against the back bumper and tapped her fingers on the lid. "I have books in the box, Daddy, and puzzles." Her eyes glinted. "We can play games, and you can help me read. It'll be so fun."

"Sure will, sweetheart." He grinned, but something inside him buckled. Could he be the father she wanted…and needed? So many duties he'd never had to handle would now be his—dental and doctor's appointments, illnesses, shopping for her clothes and being a good role model. The list overwhelmed him.

When he glanced up, Renee stood at the door watching. They'd covered everything on the phone, so she had no need to go over it now. He closed the trunk and slipped into the car, waiting while Kaylee latched her seat belt, and her face beamed as she waved goodbye. Renee didn't appear as happy as Kaylee. He put himself in her shoes and understood. Kaylee had been a big part of her life. Could he measure up to Renee?

"Do Ashley and Joey know that I live with you now?"

Her question broke his thoughts. "Not yet. They got home last night, but we'll tell them today."

"I can't wait." She swung her feet, kicking the back of the passenger seat.

He couldn't wait, either. His shoulders relaxed, listening to Kaylee chatter in the backseat.

"Daddy?"

"What, sweetie?"

"Joey's birthday's soon. He'll be four and I'm four." Her voice lilted with happiness.

"That's right." Apparently the old age issue had faded.

"But I'm almost five so I'm still bigger."

He chuckled. "You are...a little. What do you think Joey would like for his birthday? Clothes. Books. Toys."

"Puzzles. He loves puzzles. Me, too, but I

don't think I need presents when I have my birthday in January."

"No presents?" Her comment surprised him. "Why? I thought you loved presents."

"I do, but I got my present already. I'm living with you."

He wanted to hold her in his arms and give her a big hug. "Hearing you say that is the best present I've had in a long time." Today being a father heightened his awareness of the joy but also the responsibility. It felt different somehow, knowing something as simple as her bedroom was really her room and not a guest room. A smile stretched his taut cheeks and her singing made him chuckle.

When they rolled down Drayton, he braked to pull into the driveway, but Kaylee blasted a command that made him jump. "Go to Ashley's house. I want to tell her I'm living with you."

He halted the car in the street. "First, say please. Second, don't yell and scare me."

"Sorry." Her tone held an apology.

"I know you're excited, but don't you want to unpack first?"

"Later. Remember what you always tell

me. When you want to do something and I ask what about unpacking, you always say my things will still be there when we get home."

He looked over the seat, and her expression made him chuckle. "I guess I do tell you that, don't I?"

She grinned and gave him a nod.

Though he'd love to see Ashley, what he needed was a nap, but he decided to listen to Kaylee's plea. He straightened the wheel and continued down three houses to Ashley's, hoping she was up and ready for company.

When he pulled into her driveway, no little nose pressed against the windowpane. He climbed out and waited for Kaylee to unhook her seat belt and slip outside before he hit the lock button. She bounded up the porch stairs and hit the doorbell before he reached the steps.

In a moment, the door opened, and Ashley's frown turned to a grin. "Kaylee. Good morning."

She stood back with only a glance at him as she eyed Kaylee. "Why are you so happy?"

Kaylee darted into the room and spun around. "I live with my daddy now!"

"You do?" Joy filled her face. "Wonderful." She leaned down and gave Kaylee a hug. "I know your daddy's happy, too, and so am I."

Before Ashley misunderstood, Devon dropped the bombshell. "It's temporary."

Ashley drew back, her eyes narrowed, brow furrowed. "But I thought—"

"It's a long story. Probably not as long as it is complex." He hoped she'd invite him to have a seat.

She didn't move. "I'm surprised that you settled for—"

"It's not settling." Her judgment sliced through him. "I said it's complex."

Finally, she motioned to a chair. "Where are my manners? Please, sit and tell me what happened."

His attention shifted to Kaylee who'd already plopped onto the sofa, all ears.

He scanned the room. "Where's Joey?"

"Upstairs. He was playing, but I think he fell asleep. He needs to get up or he'll be awake all night." She turned to Kaylee. "Would you run up and check on him?"

Kaylee slipped from the sofa and headed up the stairs, appearing proud she had an important assignment.

Relieved, he wanted to make good use of the time alone with Ashley. He sank onto the sofa, which Kaylee had vacated. "Renee wouldn't make the decision. She said it was up to Gina." He shrugged. "In part she's right, but who knows what Gina will say. She's very defensive, but I learned one thing. She's spent more time in the hospital than out of it lately."

"Did Renee tell you that?"

"No, I said it to her and she didn't deny it." He grinned at the way he'd gathered information she might never have told him.

"Good for you, Devon. Smart."

"But the worst thing I learned..." He checked the staircase. Empty. "Gina tried to commit suicide. I'm thinking this isn't the first time."

Ashley's gasp preceded the horror on her face. "That's awful. Terrible."

He could only nod.

"Wasn't she a Christian, Devon? I assumed she—"

"Gina's the one who led me to faith. I wasn't a churchgoer before I met her. I don't understand her illness, but I think her values and beliefs have been damaged by her mental state. I pray the Lord doesn't hold that against someone who is truly ill."

Ashley leaned forward, her head swaying from side to side. "I'm not blaming Gina or condemning her, Devon. Not one bit. Remember we're not to judge lest we be judged. I try to follow that."

Weight lifted from his shoulders. "I hope you're right, Ash." Hearing her nickname from his lips startled him. She didn't seem to notice, but using it brought her closer, more familiar than her formal name.

Ashley rose from her chair and resettled beside him. She slipped her hand into his. "Devon, I believe that we have a loving God. He sees us as pure and blessed. How could a loving God condemn a faithful Christian whose mind has warped and led her astray.

God is the judge and He is forgiving and loving. What more do we need?"

He weaved his fingers through hers, wanting to draw her into his arms. "Thanks. I should know that, but I needed the reminder." Touched by her tenderness, he leaned over and kissed her.

She turned her face toward him, her eyes giving him permission, and her lips met his again. His heart soared. Hope escalated. Though he needed sleep—needed it badly—he sensed today was the day to pursue their conversation cut short by Neely's call a few days earlier.

A noise from the upper floor caught Devon's attention. He patted Ashley's hand and headed for the staircase. "What are you doing, Kaylee?"

"Joey's up, and we're playing." She appeared on the landing. "He dropped a truck."

Devon glanced at Ashley. "Is it okay for them to play up there?"

"Sure. It's fine." She nodded, a smile growing on her face.

His stomach tightened at the grin as well as the knowledge they had more time alone.

"Kaylee, be good up there. Don't get into anything."

"I won't." She gave him a minifrown as if insulted at his suggestion she might get into something. He had to admit, other than looking into the photo albums without permission, Kaylee minded well.

He turned away and settled beside Ashley, his hopes growing. "How was your visit with Paula? Difficult, I suppose."

"In some ways, yes." She leaned her back against the cushion, but her hand rested on his knee. "We weren't close to Aunt Florence after Mother died. She wasn't the most pleasant hostess. Neely and I felt sorry for Paula. She was an only child, so she had little camaraderie."

"Sad." Though he was an only child, his parents had been loving people.

"Neely and I understood when she left home so young. Paula moved out right after high school. Went to college and never came back except for holidays."

A strange look grew on her face, and he suspected something else had happened while they were gone. "Something's wrong."

A frown curved her mouth. "Not really. I—" She shook her head. "I'm just thinking."

"About your mother?"

Her head hitched back, questioning filling her eyes. "What do you mean?"

"I was here when you got the call. I know you wondered if Paula could tell you more about your mother's earlier years." He tilted his head, weighing her expression. "Am I wrong?"

She lowered her eyes. "No." She sat a moment before looking up. "But it's personal, and I'm not sure I should talk about it."

Though curious, he knew his place. "Not if you think it's wrong. If you feel like talking, I'm a willing listener."

She lifted her gaze, moisture filling her eyes. The story spilled from her, at least what she knew, and though it left more doors open, the truth seemed obvious. The two women had been sexually abused as girls.

"I can understand why you feel sad, Ashley."

"I'm sad my mother had to endure the horrors of her uncle, but I'm even sadder that she let someone else's sin ruin her life. She carried the guilt and degradation as if it had been her doing."

"Sometimes people blame themselves. In abuse cases, women sometimes think they asked for it by their dress or behavior. It's tragic, because the cause had nothing to do with your mother or your aunt. The cause was a predator who took advantage, made them lose self-worth and the power to do something about it."

"You're right, Devon." She leaned forward and rested her head on his chest. "My mother's feelings of unworthiness caused her to belittle us so she could convince herself she had value. Not only were my mother's and aunt's lives ruined, but their children's lives, as well. We missed the joy of having a mother who expressed her love and provided a warm, comfortable home for her girls. Everyone was cheated."

Ashley's story pained him. His own self-doubts had nearly ruined his life, too, but somehow knowing her had opened the doors and turned his life around. Losing Ashley would undo him.

A sigh rattled from his chest, and he fought to keep his eyes from closing.

"You're exhausted."

"I only got a little sleep last night. I would have slept better, but Kaylee was on my mind."

"And the situation with Gina."

She knew him well. "Yes. That, too."

She slid her arm around his back. "Go home and take a nap. I'll entertain Kaylee. She can have lunch here, and we can get together later."

Her eyes searched his, but he couldn't decide what to do. So much depended on their talk, but Ashley was right. He needed sleep.

She curved her palm against his cheek and turned his face to hers. Her lips moved toward his and captured his mouth, a kiss he had only dreamed about.

Devon shifted, drawing her closer, her mouth warm, his heart slamming against his breastbone.

Ashley drew back, a sweet expression on her face. She managed to rise and held her hands toward him.

He grasped them and rose, his focus on

her. He loved her. No denying it. But he could never tell her until he was certain she felt the same.

She squeezed his hands. "A nap first. Then we talk."

Balancing hope with despair, he nodded. "We must."

Ashley tiptoed up and brushed her lips across his again. "Yes."

With his expectations mounting, he managed to call up to Kaylee that he'd see her later and made it outside before Ashley's yes turned on him. If the two sentences congealed—*yes...we must* could mean anything. We must open our hearts to each other, or we must end this relationship and say goodbye.

His spirit sagging, he drove home and prayed he could sleep.

Chapter Fourteen

Ashley leaned against the recliner wishing she'd talked things out with Devon earlier. The delay preyed on her mind, and the day crumbled into dust. She couldn't concentrate on anything. She'd kept her eyes on the kids, fed them lunch and looked through magazines, but her thoughts stayed on Devon. She couldn't say goodbye, and she couldn't make a commitment.

She'd thought about calling him. The waiting dragged on until she thought she'd scream, but she restrained the desire and prayed instead that the Lord be with them during their conversation.

Only two other things hung on the fringe

of her mind. One was Joey's upcoming birthday, but the one more urgent event was her sister's wedding. Though both occasions needed attention, the wedding was in less than two weeks. She gazed at her cast. Her next appointment with the surgeon left her hoping the clunky thing would be removed.

"Mama."

Ashley straightened her back, then rose and went to the staircase. "What, Joey?"

"Can we play outside?"

She heard Kaylee's voice saying something about the park and waited for Joey to finish.

"Can we play in the park?"

"You can play outside, but not in the park. Maybe when Devon comes."

Silence.

She returned to her chair. At the park, she'd enjoy the fresh air, and the kids would be busy on the swings and slides. She and Devon would have a little alone time. The thought ended with the clomp of footsteps on the stairs. Kaylee appeared at the bottom followed by Joey.

"We'll go outside until Daddy comes."

Ashley gave her approval and listened until

the side door closed. She leaned back into the recliner, the wait yawning in front of her.

Looking through the wide front window, she saw Kaylee at the foot of the driveway pulling Joey in his wagon. Kaylee turned and headed along the sidewalk. When she was out of sight, Ashley lowered the footrest and stood, but her fear vanished when Kaylee returned heading in the other direction. She sank into the chair, wondering if she would ever stop worrying about Joey.

A car door's slam brought her to attention again, and Devon strode down the driveway to greet the kids. He gave them both a hug, his attention mostly on Kaylee, who no doubt told him they were going to the park.

Whatever he said appeased her for the moment. Ashley listened for the doorknob to turn, and when it did, he strutted in, giving her a wink. "I see Kaylee's planned our afternoon."

"Joey was part of the plan, I think." She rose again, heading toward him. "I hope you don't mind I agreed."

"Not at all." He opened his arms to her.

Although he grinned, he seemed anxious.

She stepped into his embrace. He held her tight for a moment, but not long enough to assure her all was well. "Did you eat?"

He nodded. "Threw a slice of meat loaf on wheat bread. Leftovers come in handy." Motioning toward the door, he took a step backward. "Ready to go?"

A shrug escaped her. "Ready as I'll ever be." She'd uttered more truth than she meant to.

He opened the door, and she followed, now making her way with more ease on the walking cast.

The kids clamored into the car, and Devon headed down Drayton toward Woodward. Though the kids chattered in the backseat, she and Devon remained silent. She tried to organize the muddle of thoughts crashing in her head. Positive feelings careened against the negative possibilities. Relief came when Devon pulled into the parking lot. She climbed out and helped Joey unhook his seat belt. Kaylee hopped to the ground on the other side and followed Devon around the car to meet them.

The playground was close, just past the

roller-hockey field, and loosened from their restraints, they darted toward the playground. Devon hurried ahead of her as she trudged along with her cast. Kaylee climbed the ladder to the slide and shot down while Devon caught up with Joey and made sure he could handle the ladder. Her heart constricted, observing the love he had for her son.

How could she doubt Devon's affection? But the situation had nothing to do with doubting Devon. It had to do with doubting herself.

Devon watched a moment and then strode to her side. He slipped his hand into hers and led her a few yards away to a picnic bench in the pavilion, empty since it was a weekday. They sat, eyes on the children but her mind on their talk. Devon sighed and she realized she wasn't the only one worried about their relationship. "What are you thinking?"

"What I always have on my mind." He shifted his eyes toward hers for a moment before redirecting them to the children as they moved to the swings. "I'm thinking about you."

The admission wasn't what she'd expected. "I thought you had Gina on your mind and the physical custody issue you have to deal with when she's out of the hospital."

"Sometimes, but that's not what scares me."

She filled in the blanks. "You're worried about me."

"In a way, yes. If you want me to be honest, I'm nervous about this talk." He rested his hand on hers. "I try to understand you, but I don't. Maybe I'm just bad at reading women's emotions."

"Mine aren't easy to read, Devon. I don't understand them, either." She inverted her palm and weaved her fingers through his.

"Then that doesn't make the job easy, does it?" He gave her a plaintive grin and squeezed her hand. "Let's start with basics." He turned his face to hers. "I think the world of you. I can't picture living without you." He quieted a moment as if in thought. "I don't want to scare you, but I need you to know my intentions. I'd like us to see where our relationship can go."

She looked into his eyes, her pulse charging through her, her heart in her throat. This was a time for honesty, if she could only find it. "I understand your feelings. My heart turns to mush when I watch you with Joey. You're loving and caring. You'd make a good father, and I never doubted you would be a wonderful husband. Never."

His head snapped up, his eyes probing hers.

She dug deeper. "I know you questioned whether Gina's problems were your lack of attention, caring, love…a multitude of questions that filled you with confusion. I never believed you lacked any of those attributes. I sensed the kind of man you were within a couple days of knowing you."

He shifted on the bench, his knees touching hers, his eyes seeking her heart. "Then what is it, Ashley? What causes you to back away sometimes? It frightens me, and I can't find a reason."

"It's not you. The problem is what you do. Firefighting." She'd said it. Finally. She'd admitted aloud the deep horrible terror that she faced daily since she admitted her feelings for him. "It's the fear, Devon. That's it. Nothing more, and it's something you can't fix or change. I would never think of asking you to leave a career that means the world to you. It would destroy the generous, loving person that you are. I will not be responsible."

"I know the hours are bad, but the days off together have their advantage. I can—"

Her heart sank. "It's not the hours you work." Her lungs constricted, leaving her nearly unable to speak. "It's the job. You lay your life on the line every day. Even now when I hear sirens, I think the worst. I wait for a call from a firefighter or one arriving at my door with sad eyes and telling me you were badly hurt or killed in a fire. I lived that experience once before, Devon, and I can't do it again."

A deep sadness permeated his face. "You're right. I can't change that. I can't fix it. If I work anywhere, you would worry that I had a car accident on the way to work. Or on the way home."

"That's different. I realize people take a chance whenever—"

His hand slipped from hers. "Ashley. You were injured by a tree falling on you in your yard. How often does that happen?"

Her pulse skipped, understanding his point. "I don't know. It's not a daily occurrence, but if I worked for a tree removal service, it would be more likely."

"You're wrong. Those men learn how to remove a tree and stay safe. Do you know how much training I've had to be a firefighter? How much training I still receive? Do you know how many fires I've helped put out, how many lives I've saved, and I don't have a scar on my body?" He leaned closer, his gaze glued to hers. "I know firefighters give their lives, but we all die eventually, Ashley. We won't live on this earth forever."

"I know, but—" He pressed a finger against her lips.

"This is where faith plays a part in our lives. God is in charge of every moment, Ash. You're the staunch Christian. You should know that. He gave us free will to make choices, but He also gave us opportunities to learn the right things to do, and He will only let us go when it's time. Adam's time had come. If he'd remained home and never joined the army, God wanted him at that time. Accidents happen. Diseases are contracted. We all leave this earth one way or the other in God's time."

Her mind reeled with his arguments. He made sense. What she needed was faith. Trust. The words from Proverbs filled her mind. *Trust in the Lord with all your heart and lean not on your own understanding.* She'd tried to make it her prayer, but she'd failed.

"Devon." She clasped both his hands. "You're right. I know it's senseless fear. I need to trust and to strengthen my faith."

Sadness filled his eyes. "I can't do that for you, Ash."

"I know. I'm the only one who can fix me. I don't know if I can fix me, but I want to change. Will you—"

He loosened his hand and slipped his arm around her. "I'll do everything I can. I'll pray with you. I'll be patient. I'll wait, Ash, because you're worth every moment."

Tears blurred her eyes, but she blinked them away. She shifted her gaze to the children. They had returned to the slides, now a tube slide wide enough for them to slide down together.

She watched the kids while Devon's words about faith and trust began building a fortress against fear. She would fight the haunting visions. Confident God brought this man into her life, she could defeat her fears.

She lifted her lips to his, and he met them, his arms drawing her close, his heart beating against hers. As their kiss deepened, her heart melted and hope rose, offering her a second chance at love.

Devon stared into the closet at his pitiful tie rack strung with three ties—all he owned. Suits and ties could never beat out his preference for casual attire. He spent most days in his navy blue uniform and work boots. At home, jeans and a T-shirt or knit polo shirt eased his stressful life.

But tonight the wedding called for appropriate attire, and despite his aversion to ties and suits, he wanted to meet Ashley's expectations. He dragged a gray tie with a purple stripe from the rack and held it against his gray pants. Good choice. After manipulating a Windsor knot beneath his collar, he slipped on his suit jacket and appraised himself in the mirror. Not bad if he did say so himself.

He chuckled at his silly gawking. Meeting Ashley had changed him. Sadly, with Gina, he'd never worried about what he wore. Gina didn't care about much of anything after a year of marriage. The lovely woman who'd intrigued him became someone he didn't know. She'd lost interest in life, and so had he. One day followed another, and life became as exciting as marching up a steep hill going nowhere. The difference between the two billowed like a cold wind blowing the dead leaves away and revealing a field of flowers shimmering in the sun.

A sigh rattled from him, grieving for the lost life he and Gina had experienced. Why did illness sneak up and sever joy from their life together? He shook his head, unwilling to devote time to sadness. Hope had burst into his life in the form of a lovely woman and her three-year-old son.

Each day since their talk, Ashley confounded him with her new outlook. Her actions proved her follow-through on the trust and faith issues. His hope for their relationship grew with each day. With Ashley in his life, a suit and tie would be his gift of love. He might grow to like it. He gave the mirror another glance before heading down the stairs.

Glad that Renee had welcomed Kaylee there for the night, he had no worries about her care. Neely had asked Joey to be the ring bearer, and Devon couldn't wait to see the boy dressed in his tux. The Wellses, Ashley's next-door neighbors, had invited Joey to spend the night with them following the wedding.

But the best news for Ashley was the removal of her walking cast. She had to be careful—her surgeon suggested she use a cane—but knowing her, Devon already knew a cane would be out of the question. He'd prayed the Lord make her leg strong and free from pain.

He locked the side door, climbed into the car and headed toward the church. By the time he pulled into the parking lot, numerous guests had already arrived. He slipped from the car and headed inside, wishing he could see Ashley before the ceremony. She'd refused to let him see her gown, and the anticipation never left him. The bride and attendants had agreed to dress at the church, so Ashley had arrived earlier.

Fred, dressed in a tuxedo, greeted him at the back of the church. "I see you escaped wearing a monkey suit." He extended his hand.

Devon chuckled as he grasped it. "This getup is enough for me."

"But you look pretty good." Fred gave him a wink. "I think my daughter will be impressed." He turned to a woman standing not far off. "Paula." He beckoned to her.

Hearing her name, Devon knew she was the cousin who'd recently lost her mother. For some reason, he'd expected her to be an older woman, but from her appearance, he guessed she was about Neely's age.

"Paula, this is Ashley's…friend." Fred turned to Devon. "Paula is the girls' cousin."

The awkward pause reminded him at the moment that's what he was. Ashley's friend. "Hi, Paula."

She smiled and clasped his hand as an usher approached and encouraged them to find a seat as if they were a couple. Paula took the usher's arm and Devon followed. They settled close to the front, and to be polite he asked Paula about her trip to Ferndale. She told him about her mother's death and the work she had to do preparing the house for sale.

The more he listened, the question popped into his mind. She'd mentioned her apartment and that made him wonder why she didn't keep the house and live there, but then he recalled the poor relationship she'd had with her mother, and the question answered itself. Sometimes closing the past proved a healthier choice than keeping it open.

The statement struck him. Instead of dwelling on his life with Gina, he would be healthier to close the door and open a new one. Looking back would get him nowhere.

Paula unfolded the wedding program, and he followed her to help pass the time. When organ music broke the murmur of voices, guests peered over their shoulders, anticipating the appearance of the wedding party. He kept his eyes forward, knowing Ashley would follow the bridesmaids.

A side door opened and Jon entered the sanctuary with three groomsmen behind him. They turned and faced the wedding guests. The organ music grew, and in his peripheral vision, he spotted the flash of dark pink. He turned his head and watched a woman glide down the aisle carrying a bouquet of pink flowers. Another attendant followed as his pulse stirred. He turned, anticipating Ashley's entrance.

He spotted her in the doorway, her gown the color of a rich red wine with the same iridescence. She held flowers the same color as her dress along with some pink ones. His heart stood still as she neared. Her long dark waves brushed against her nearly bare shoulders. The dress was sleeveless with a scoop neckline and fell in soft pleats to the floor. He closed his eyes picturing her in a pastel bridal gown, gliding down the aisle to join her groom. The image warmed him, yet behind the hope, he still faced a cold possibility. She'd promised to try. Try left a lot of leeway.

Though his attention remained on Ashley, the oohs echoing from the back caused him to turn again. A young girl, perhaps Kaylee's age, sprinkled flower petals along the white runner while Joey walked beside her, carrying a shiny white pillow. Devon's chest expanded and a sense of pride ballooned inside him. When Joey saw him, he lifted his hand to wave, and Devon's heart stopped as he watched the pillow tip to the side. Joey's grin faded to terror, but he caught it before it and the ring tumbled to the floor. Devon breathed again, a grin growing on his face.

The music swelled, and the guests rose as Neely floated down the aisle. His mind replaced her face with Ashley's, and he closed his eyes to chase away the vision. That kind of thinking would only dig the hole deeper if Ashley failed to resolve her issues.

As she joined Jon, the congregation sat, and the ceremony began, a mixture of vows and prayers, but through it all, he relived the vows he'd made years earlier, despite his thought to let the door close on the past. He'd made a vow to God that had been broken, but regret could never undo what had been done. Only God could forgive and offer him another door, and he sensed that door had opened, today dressed in a claret gown that glinted in the candlelight.

His focus on Ashley, the wedding kiss ended the ceremony, but he forced his attention on Neely and Jon as they returned down the aisle, man and wife. Ashley followed along with Joey, and he waited as the ushers released the rows of guests, longing to take Ashley in his arms and breathe in the scent of her soft skin.

Paula chatted, saying how great it was to be with family and a little about Roscommon, and though he was distracted, he managed to converse and make sense. At least he tried. He strode down the line of attendants, offering smiles and nods, and when he came to Fred, he was introduced to Jon's parents, making him aware that Ashley had never met his.

When he finally reached Ashley, his heartbeat thudded against his chest. He clasped her hand. "You look amazing."

She ran her finger down his tie. "So do you." A playful frown slid to her face. "How did you know to wear a tie with a maroon chevron?" Then she grinned. "We match. Did you notice?"

He glanced at the stripe in his gray tie, surprised that she was right. "Just talented, I guess." Though he appeared lighthearted, he wrestled his longing to kiss her.

"I'll see you at the reception." She tilted her head, her expression sorry. "We have to stick around for the photos, and you know the tradition."

"Driving around tooting the horn?"

She nodded and gave his hand a squeeze.

He congratulated Neely and Jon, then moved to the door, where he paused and watched Ashley greeting other guests. Her smiles and vibrancy riddled his emotions. She left no doubt in his mind. He loved her. He absolutely loved her.

Ashley climbed from the car, careful to put the most weight on her good leg. The joy of having the cast removed equaled the happiness she felt for Neely and Jon. They made a perfect couple, and she couldn't ask for a better brother-in-law than Jon. The bonus was, they both enjoyed Devon's company.

Each day Devon's generosity overwhelmed her. He'd waited for a few wedding photos that included Joey and then hoisted him up—two handsome men grinning at her— and drove him to the Wellses for the night. Great neighbors and Devon, a greater friend.

"Friend" sounded feeble. Their friendship had become more important than she could ever imagine, since the day she looked into his worried face from beneath the tree limbs. He'd grown as close as her right arm. Life would never be the same without him, and she knew he'd become far more than a typical friend. Her heartbeat pulsed, recalling how amazing he looked in his gray suit and the perfect tie.

Neely's appearance at her side startled her. The new bride wore a silly grin on her face. "You're thinking about him, aren't you?"

"Him?" She tried to play dumb, but Neely knew better. She'd confided in her sister more than once, and Neely was the first to congratulate her on taking a step of faith away from her widow's life.

Neely shook her head. "Anyone who knows you can see you're in love."

Though her heart knew the truth, hearing the words gave her a chill. "Did you ever think you'd be filled with wedding thoughts? Love means commitment, and—" She released a stream of air. "And I need your prayers for that."

"You've had them for months, Ash."

Jon slipped beside her, and Neely's attention flew away, but Ashley knew her sister understood.

Inside the hall, they waited for the deejay to introduce the bridal party and then the bride and groom. The many wedding traditions had meant a lot to her when she married Adam, but today they seemed somewhat pointless. Marriage was far more than a tossed bouquet and bridal dance. Weddings were a sacred union between a man and woman. On that day, they joined together and promised God nothing could part them except death. She'd lived that life, and she realized that vow was what Devon struggled with. If Gina had been faithful to her vows, they would still be married today. A chill tingled down her back.

The music played and both of Neely's

bridesmaids were on the dance floor with a groomsman. Dale, Jon's best man, stepped beside her. "Ready?" A look of concern filled his face. "Are you sure your leg can take this?"

She nodded. "We'll be careful."

He smiled and led her toward the dance floor as their names were called. Dale stood true to his word as he eased her around the floor until the bride and groom were called for the bridal dance. With Neely and Jon whirling in the center to their song "The Way You Look Tonight," Dale guided her to the side and instead of dancing, they stood swaying to the music.

A familiar fragrance wafted past her, and her pulse skipped as Devon appeared at her side. Dale nodded, aware of their relationship, and moved toward his wife.

Devon slipped his arm around her waist. "Want to dance a slow one?"

"With you, anytime." Completeness eased into every crevice of her body. For years, she felt only half-full. Tonight she felt whole.

His hand moved, glided across her back

to the dance floor and then returned to her waist. "What is this gown made of?"

"You like it?"

He nodded. "It feels like warm ice."

The imagery made her chuckle. "It's dupioni. In English, it's silk, an iridescent silk. I love it, too."

He nestled her closer and she longed to kiss him.

When the deejay opened the dance floor to everyone, Devon drew her into an embrace and guided her into the crowd, where they glided side to side, an easy sway to protect her leg. She could see his concern.

She squeezed his hand. "My leg is fine. I think I can even spin."

His frown flickered and then faded. He slipped his toe beneath her shoe, lifting her feet from the floor, and twirled her around. The sensation rolled through her like a warm breeze. He'd given her spring again. The winter of her life had passed.

As the song segued to a faster one, Devon steered her away from the dancers, and knowing dinner was a ways off, she drew him toward a set of French doors and beck-

oned him to follow. When they stepped outside, the scent of roses greeted them and the
day's warmth still hung on the air. "What do
you think?"

He looked around in the dimming light.
"It's nice. Quiet. Peaceful."

She chuckled. "I meant the view."

He grasped her hands and faced her, holding her out at arm's length. "The view is
amazing."

Heat rose up her neck, and with the scoop
top, she could guarantee he noticed her flush.
"I meant the garden."

"It's pretty, but what I'm looking at is mag-
nificent. Your hair looks amazing with the
purple dress."

"It's burgundy or maroon." She rested her
index finger on his tie. "The same as the
stripe."

"Maybe claret. Like wine."

"I think you're right." She chuckled, realizing how mundane yet enjoyable their silly
conversation was—like comfy slippers. She
glanced over her shoulder, wishing they had
more time alone. "I think they're getting
ready for dinner. We should go back."

"We'll come out here later when the stars are in the sky." He brushed the side of his hand along her cheek.

Her heart swelled at his touch.

Inside she sat at the bridal table eating her meal but longing to be at her dad's table with Paula and Devon. She watched Paula converse with him, and a wave of envy washed over her. Silly, she knew, but seeing him laugh with another woman made everything real. She eyed her empty finger where the wedding band she'd worn until recently had finally found a home in her dresser drawer, her first step toward facing the truth.

Another awareness opened her eyes. Paula was attractive. She'd never noticed when they were cousin talking to cousin. In Roscommon, she'd witnessed stress on Paula's face during the visitation and funeral and later talking about the details she had to handle to close the estate. Tonight the stress had faded, and her face glowed in the twinkle of the candles on each table.

The best man's toast ended with applause and the clink of glasses, and she knew her time had come. She rose, thanking everyone for attending, sharing some humorous moments in their lives as sisters, and then said what was in her heart. "But no matter what silly threats we screamed at each other as girls, Neely has become my best friend. When I need her, she's always there, helping me through the direst time of my life, being a loving auntie to Joey, and one of the best people I know. Today brings a new chapter in her life with a bonus. Now I have two best friends who'll stand by me. Jon, I couldn't ask for a better brother or friend. Welcome to our family, and I pray God gives you lots of children so I can take my turn babysitting."

The guests roared and struck their spoons against their water goblets, encouraging Neely and Jon to kiss. They did to a round of applause, and Ashley returned to her seat, grateful that most of her responsibilities had ended.

When she was able to leave the bride's table, she made her way to Devon standing near the glass wall, looking outside. As she approached him, the chandelier and table's candle centerpieces reflected in the glass, distorting the view. But when Devon opened the door, she stepped outside to a dark sky dotted with stars and a crescent moon. He slipped his arm around her waist, keeping her footing solid on the flagstone walk. Beyond a border of shrubs, he pointed to a bench nestled near a flower bed brimming with blossoms.

She sat, and he settled beside her, his arm again around her back, holding her close. "Great night."

"Especially now." She tilted her head and captured his eyes. He read her silent words. He drew closer, his lips on hers. As she moved with a tender touch, her mind swirled with thoughts she wanted to share, yet fought the fear of saying them.

When he drew back, his gaze stayed on hers.

"I've been thinking." His arm tensed, and she was sorry she'd begun that way. "Thinking about us, and—"

His eyes filled with question.

"Good things about us." She touched his cheek. "I want to make this work, Devon. I'm dealing with my unreasonable fears. So many things you said that day made sense.

Accidents happen no matter where we are. Home. In our cars. On a plane. Or on the job. Anytime. Anyplace. Ferndale, Michigan or some desert in Afghanistan. My foolish worries and negative outlook destroys good possibilities and only reflects my lack of faith, and I don't want it to be like that. I want to be trusting and faith-filled."

"That's what I want, too, Ash. And I see the difference in you. I know you're working on it, and I couldn't ask for more." He rose and drew her up into his embrace, his heart beating against hers. "Does this mean we're a real couple? More than friends?"

"We've been more than friends for a long time. I just had to admit it."

"I love when you admit it."

"So do I." His lips captured hers again, and in the light of the moon and stars, her heart soared into the summer air. Tonight she felt strong. Nothing could destroy what they had. Nothing.

Chapter Fifteen

Devon grinned as he thought about Ashley's enthusiasm over Joey's birthday. The day they had shopped for the boy's gifts opened another new door. Maneuvering through crowds in a mall had always fallen somewhere near the bottom of his list of things to do, but on that day with Ashley's hand in his, the task had moved up in the ranks at an astonishing pace. Even the thought of wearing a suit and tie added new meaning to the idea of dressing up. The look in her eyes the night of the wedding made it all worthwhile.

Their talk in the garden replayed in his head. Though the stars and moon added to the atmosphere, he sensed God at work that night when Ashley bared her heart and admitted all that he'd wanted to hear. Each day with her in his life had become a gift.

But today gifts belonged to Joey. Devon looked at him sitting in the "birthday boy" chair, as Ashley called it, surrounded by his gifts, most already opened, though he still had a couple more surprises. When he spied the box Devon had brought in, Joey flung the paper aside and beamed at the numerous miniature vehicles—automobiles, police cars, an EMT truck and even a fire engine. He lifted his gaze toward Devon and grasped the fire truck. "Is this like yours?"

Devon controlled a chuckle. "Just like it, but lots bigger."

"Bigger." He nodded. "So you fit inside."

"Me and a few other firefighters." The interest on the boy's face spurred him on. "One day I'll take you to the firehouse. You can see a truck close up."

Joey's eyes widened and a gigantic grin flew to his face. "Let's go now." He dropped the miniature engine and slipped off the chair. "Can I sit in the truck?"

Ashley came to the rescue. "Another time,

young man. You still have a present…or two, and we have ice cream and cake."

That did the trick, and he slipped back onto the chair, his eyes sweeping the area for the second gift. He noticed the one Kaylee held.

She grinned. "This is from me." She handed it to him.

As he tore off the paper, his face lit up. "Puzzles." He held up a box cover and showed the photo of three kittens in a basket. Apparently forgetting about the second gift his mother mentioned, he plopped to the floor and tried to lift the lid. "Kaylee, we can do puzzles now."

Ashley confiscated the gift. "Let's finish your last gift and then you can play."

Though his expression pointed to his confusion, Joey arose from the floor and stood beside Kaylee, who appeared to prefer putting together the puzzles than see the other gift.

Devon scooted out of the room and hurried to the backdoor where he'd hidden the last surprise. When he wheeled it through the archway, Joey could hardly contain himself. He darted to the new bicycle with trainer wheels and tried to hug it. "A new bike." He spun around to face his mother. "It's a real bike for me."

"What do you say to Devon?" She gave him the eye.

"I say let's go outside."

Everyone laughed, though he missed the point until Kaylee told him to say thank-you.

Ashley gave him a hug. "Now, how about some cake and ice cream?"

Kaylee followed Ashley to the kitchen, but Joey stood in the middle of the room, still mesmerized by his gifts. He turned from the bike to the miniature cars to the puzzles as if overwhelmed with his decision about which one to play with first.

Ashley called from the kitchen for them to find seats in the dining room.

Devon took Joey's hand and guided him toward the treats. Joey scampered ahead, and before Devon could sit, his cell phone rang. He tugged it from his breast pocket and saw Renee's name. "I'll be right back." He held up his finger and retreated to the living room. "What's up?"

"Gina's home."

As soon as he heard Renee's voice, he realized they had a problem. "She's upset?"

"That's only part of it."

He waited for more, but all he heard was silence. "Please tell me what's going on."

"She's not well. They should have kept her. The hallucinations are worse than when she left."

Renee hadn't told him about those. "What kind of hallucinations?" His pulse escalated as his concern grew.

"She's bipolar, Devon. You knew that, right?"

"You mean now. Is this a new problem? She wasn't bipolar before." His cheek ticked with tension.

"Sorry, but she did. She had tendencies, but her medication kept things under control. If she stopped taking them, then the condition got worse."

He froze to the spot. "Gina never explained what it was for. She said the pills were for her nerves. I never questioned her, Renee. I didn't realize…" He closed his eyes, recalling she'd had to stop taking the pills when she became pregnant. "If I'd known—"

"It's not your fault. Gina refused to discuss her diagnosis. She insisted she was fine, but now we know that wasn't the case. The psychologist told me that she has a tendency toward schizophrenia, and that's not good news."

The word jarred Devon. "It's dangerous."

"She hears a voice telling her to do things. Take her life is one of things they tell her."

"What can you… We do?" His mind spun. Concern for Kaylee's safety surged through his mind. He imagined what the voice might tell her to do. He pressed his fingers against his temple, wishing away the thunder in his brain. "Is she okay with Kaylee living here?"

"She wants to see her, Devon. I haven't told her that she's staying with you for more than your days off." She released a stream of air. "Can you bring her home?"

His spine straightened. "She is home, Renee. Remember?"

"But…"

"I'll talk with her, but not today. We're at a birthday party, and it's not a good time."

"Do you think it's a good time for me?"

"No." He rubbed his hand across his

mouth, asking the Lord to give him words that were filled with kindness and not the ones on the tip of his tongue. "Tomorrow. I'll get there tomorrow alone, and later I'll bring Kaylee, but I need to talk to Gina first."

Kaylee darted through the archway and skidded to a stop. "Daddy, we want to sing 'Happy Birthday' to Joey."

"Tomorrow. That's all I can do." He gave Kaylee a nod. "I have to hang up now."

She mumbled concerns but finally said goodbye.

He hit the end call button and slipped his arm around Kaylee as they returned to the kitchen. He had no plan to tell her about the call now. In Kaylee's eyes he'd given her a gift when she came to live with him. He wouldn't take that away.

Ashley stood at her front window, straining to see down the street and to know if Devon had returned home from his visit with Gina. Her heart ached for him, but as much for herself. She'd grown to love Kaylee as her own—the thought scared her—but it was true. Having the girl stay with her while Devon worked had melded the family together like hot chocolate and marshmallows. Kaylee had fit in, becoming a playmate for Joey and a help to her.

Devon could go to court with powerful ammunition against Gina, but would he? His pure heart and concern for his former wife, as well as the impact of a court battle, could damage Kaylee. She prayed the Lord would intervene and point the way for the answer.

Her leg tired, she sank into her recliner and hoisted the footrest. Healing took time, and the last thing she wanted to do was cause problems with her leg. The memory of the day the tree fell dropped into mind with horror but also with joy. She'd met Devon, an amazing gift in her life. She'd bypassed her concern, and grasping her faith and Devon's confidence in their relationship, she'd laid down the burden and stepped into a new world promising an amazing journey.

A sound roused her, and she stood up, her focus on the window and her driveway. Disappointed, she sank back into her chair. On one hand, she'd been grateful for her dad. He'd invited the children to lunch at their favorite fast-food restaurant with a play area, but now she needed a distraction and without them nothing drew her away from waiting, not even her work.

Her contacts had grown, and with Kaylee there to entertain Joey, she'd had more time to keep up with the stacks of computer and paperwork that accumulated on her desk. Grateful for the income, she enjoyed spending time with Devon and the children far more.

One niggling thought stayed with her, a new issue she hadn't considered until recently. Joey adored Devon and carried the fire truck into his bedroom each night. Fire truck. Boys emulated their fathers. What would she do if one day Joey wanted to be a firefighter? The distant possibility seemed a ridiculous concern when she thought logically, but when her heart took over it burned in her mind.

The foolish worry was another burden she had to lay at Jesus' feet. Now that she'd opened her heart and admitted her feelings, sliding back was no longer an option. Months ago she thought nothing could pull her away from the memories of her life with Adam. They'd only shared a couple short years before the army called him away. Still, at times, it seemed like a lifetime. But her life had changed. Today, though the bittersweet memories remained, her joy covered them with new experiences and memories.

The backdoor opened, and she jumped. Her back straightened as her eyes shifted to the archway. Devon stepped into the room, his expression a muddle of emotion.

She rose and opened her arms. "Was it that bad?"

He closed his eyes and moved into her arms, clinging to her. "Let's sit."

Weariness emanated from his body, and she drew back to her chair while he sank into the easy chair nearby. "She's not the woman I married." He shook his head. She looked like an old woman, her back hunched, deep furrows around her eyes. "Whatever is going on in her body, in her head, is killing her. My heart breaks for Kaylee. She's been living with Gina as her major caregiver and has grown up seeing the shell of the mother she once had."

Tension knotted in her shoulders, and she pulled her arms back to relieve the strain. "You don't think that Gina would really take her own life, do you?"

"Her attempts so far have been waylaid, but I don't know, Ash. One day she might try and there'll be no one to stop her and get to her in time." He shook his head. "I really don't know."

"Does she realize what she'd do to Kaylee. She'd be without a mother, and—"

"She's without one now. Her body's there, but her heart and mind are so tangled in the drugs she takes and the disease that's destroyed her spirit, I don't think she's in tune to much of anything most of the time. I've never known anyone so incapacitated by an illness like this."

"It's horrible for Kaylee and you. There's so little you can do, I'm at a loss."

His eyes agreed. "She's lost so much I feel guilty taking Kaylee from her. It seems so unkind...so thoughtless."

"Kaylee asked to live with you, Devon." Her stomach knotted as she talked, and she felt sick. "You don't know if Gina will hurt herself and Kaylee will witness that." Her greatest fear was Gina would also harm Kaylee to keep them together. It wasn't unheard of with a mental illness. "Don't forget, Devon, besides being her father and her loving you, now you understand the importance of having custody."

"We talked a little, but her mind wanders. Then she'll come back to Kaylee and ask why she hadn't come with me."

"When you told her your thoughts, did she understand?"

His shoulders lifted in a heavy sigh. "I explained, but..." His head lowered. "I couldn't tell her Kaylee asked to live with me. I just couldn't."

Ashley nodded, understanding yet wishing he had. "You'll have to tell her if it comes to that."

"I know. I'm hoping it doesn't. I told her I'd bring Kaylee back when I return to work on Thursday." He lifted his head, his eyes glazed. "She fell asleep as we were talking. Renee said she sleeps much of the time."

"That's no life for—" Ashley let the sentence die. He knew it wasn't a life for Kaylee, and he didn't need to hear it again. What he needed was a solution. "Will you tell Kaylee so she's prepared?"

"I think she knows the situation better than I do, Ash." His eyes misted. "She's been watching her mother sink deeper and deeper into this sad condition. Who knows how she's coped."

"She looked forward to her days with you, I imagine." It was the first time she'd seen him look more cheerful since he'd walked through the door.

"Thanks. I'm not letting her go back. Nothing will change that."

Her spirit lifted hearing his determination. "I'm glad."

A car pulled up in front of the house, and Ashley rose and craned her neck to see who it was. "Dad's back with the kids."

He brushed at his eyes. "Good timing. I need cheering up."

The side door banged against the wall, and the children's chatter reached them. Her dad's voice followed. "We're home."

She laughed. "Good thing you're not burglars. I'd have already dialed 911."

The kids bounded into the room, both talking about what they ate and their fun in the play area. "We met Alice."

Ashley's head bobbed up with Kaylee's comment. "You took Alice with you, huh?"

He shrugged. "She likes kids, and two pairs of eyes watching them in the play area was better than one pair."

She chuckled at his excuses. Alice seemed to be in his life more than she realized. "Tell her thank-you."

"She loves it, and so do the kids. They can con her out of anything."

Ashley arched a brow, concerned. "You shouldn't let them get away with—"

He tossed his head back with a laugh. "She's like any grandma. She loves to make them happy." He wagged his hand as if wiping away her concern. "It was just ice cream."

Devon had been quiet until the last comment. "Like a grandma. Hmm? That's interesting." He gave Ashley a wink. "Is there something you're not telling us?"

Ashley chuckled when she noticed a faint

flush on her dad's face. A romance was really blooming.

"Don't start playing matchmaker, you two."

Ashley laughed out loud at that. "Tit for tat, Dad. How many times have I told you to stop matching me up with possible husbands?"

He grinned. "That's different."

She shook her head, not trying to find another barb.

Joey strode to Devon, his face tilted up to his. "Can we go to the fire station now?"

"You promised, Daddy, remember?"

Her concern vanished when she saw Devon's face brighten. He needed a distraction from his problems and making the kids happy would do that.

Devon looked at Ashley. "What do you think?"

"I think it's a great idea."

He nodded, the look reflecting the thought she'd just had. "You'll have fun. All of you."

"We will."

The kids charged toward the door, and she barely had time to say goodbye, but this goodbye was a good one, because it was also a goodbye to Devon's gloom. How could he be sad with happy kids around?

Devon smiled along with the children, their excitement evident as they scampered in front of him toward the firehouse entrance. He'd asked the captain about bringing them, but he knew the answer would be yes. Still, he wanted to make sure it was a good day, one without serious calls. Those days were precious. And so were the kids as they bounded through the door.

The guys who saw them come into the station sent him a wave. "I brought some important guests for a visit today."

His friends welcomed the kids, and he stepped back, letting them lead the tour through their living quarters, the dining room, where their eyes widened when they saw three refrigerators and the large stove. They had to be encouraged to leave the exercise room or they would have stayed there to play on the stair steps, and Joey wanted to lift weights. The boy made him laugh.

Finally they were eager to head to the apparatus area with all the firehouse gear, the rescue truck, ambulance and what Joey had been waiting for—the fire truck.

The men's patience answering questions and allowing the kids to try on the gear made Devon proud of his pals. He watched Joey's eyes shift to the engine so often, waiting for his chance to climb into the truck. When the time came, Devon's pulse gave a kick almost as happy as the kids, but before he could enjoy the experience, his cell rang. Though tempted to ignore it, he had second thoughts and eyed the caller ID. Gina.

His heart jarred before the thump struck temples. He caught a firefighter's attention and pointed to the phone. His friend nodded, and he scooted out of earshot and answered. "Gina, is something wrong?"

"I need to see her now, Devon."

He drew the phone from his ear, confused. "Why now? She's with me and one of her playmates at the firehouse."

"Now, please. It's important, and I—"

He heard Renee's voice in the background, and he sensed something very wrong. "Gina, can I talk with—"

"No, Devon. I need to see Kaylee." He'd promise to bring her there tomorrow not today. He'd have time to explain the visit to Kaylee, to prepare her at least.

Panic filled her voice and his concern rose. If she hurt herself because of his delay, he would never forgive himself. "I'll bring her within the hour."

Silence.

"Did you hear me?"

"Thank you." He heard the click of a disconnect.

He lurched hearing the desperation in Gina's voice. He hadn't wanted to tell Kaylee anything about the problem, but he knew she would ask why they had to go today.

After slipping the phone into his pocket, he hurried to the fire truck, his heart heavy with concern. He hoped Kaylee wouldn't ask, but he knew her too well. She would.

With the tour completed, Devon stepped in and used his cell phone to take a photo of Kaylee and Joey in the fire truck, and the firefighters gathered around and presented them with red firefighter hats and a junior firefighter badge. They were overjoyed.

He would have been, too, except Gina's voice grated on his conscience, along with her demand to see Kaylee now.

After thanking the men, he herded the kids to the car, his mind reeling, his concern growing. He longed to come up with a plan of action, but action against what? Gina's demand hung before him with no direction. All she'd insisted was to see Kaylee today, though the little girl still had one more day to stay with him as far as Gina knew. Renee hadn't explained the situation yet, and now that left it up to him.

When they arrived at Ashley's, Joey's and Kaylee's chatter about their visit to the firehouse droned in his ear. He had little time, and he finally distracted them enough to relay a few seconds of the conversation to Ashley before an explanation to Kaylee.

On the way home to pick up anything she needed, he had to explain. "Your mom's home. I talked with her."

Kaylee's head popped up. "When?"

"I'm not sure when she came home, but she called while you were in the fire truck."

A frown settled on her face, and she only searched his eyes in silence.

"She wants to see you now, Kaylee, so we'll take a ride there, okay?"

Her expression darkened, and she remained silent as if weighing his words. "But I can come back here." Though a question, her inflection made it sound like a statement.

"I don't know what she wants, sweetheart. We'll have to find out."

"Daddy, I…" Her voice sank with a look of despair.

He'd never seen her react this way, and his stomach knotted. Why the change? She'd never rejected her mother, and he didn't want that now, but he didn't know what she'd lived with for so long. Even a toddler senses things amiss, and Kaylee had a keen sense.

"I'll go with you. Does that help?"

The tightness of her lips softened as she nodded.

They drove in silence most of the way with only an occasional comment on her fun at the firehouse. He was sorry he'd ended her wonderful day with this news. He said a prayer that some good could come from what seemed an impossible situation.

When they pulled into the driveway, Kaylee unhooked her belt and stood outside the car as if waiting for him to stand beside her. He took her hand as they headed to the porch and when they opened the doors, Gina stood there, dark circles beneath her once-lovely eyes and gaunt flesh as pale as ash. An ache tore through his body.

He took the first step with Kaylee. "I said an hour. We're here, Gina."

"Go home, Devon. I want to spend time with my daughter alone. I'll call you tomorrow."

Panic filled Kaylee's face, her desperate look aimed at him.

His concern rose, hearing tomorrow. "You go and visit your mom, and I'll see you soon." He backed off the stair, startled by Kaylee's expression and his own desperation.

Kaylee stepped inside and the door closed without Gina saying another word. He'd expected a thank-you, but expectations only led to disappointment.

He stood a moment, catching his breath, his mind weighted with questions.

What did Gina have on her mind? What could he do to protect Kaylee from being pulled into a battle? He looked heavenward, hoping his prayer had reached the Lord.

Though he wanted to move, his fear held him fast. He couldn't leave without doing something. Renee. His option was to call her. Gina resented him, but her sister was a different story. Renee would make sure nothing happened to Kaylee and his prayer would help cinch it.

Chapter Sixteen

Ashley sat in the recliner, her eyes glued to the door, waiting for Devon to return. When his car finally pulled into the driveway, the side door opened and a lone pair of footsteps sounded on the kitchen floor.

Devon stepped through the archway, his face drained of color. "Don't ask." He sank onto the sofa and stared into the distance. "Gina wouldn't talk with me. She opened the door and dismissed me as if I were Kaylee's chauffeur. Not even a thank-you."

Any possible response seemed futile. She'd said it all before, and words seemed empty. She knew he'd begun to pray on a regular basis. She knew he didn't wish Gina ill. But she knew nothing else. Obviously Devon didn't, either.

"She's keeping Kaylee overnight." He shrugged. "That's all I know, and fighting in front of Kaylee was the last thing I wanted to do. I didn't explain that Kaylee's staying with me. I knew it would cause an uproar. Her condition is delicate. I backed away." He lowered his head. "But I had second thoughts, and I called Renee. She agreed to leave work and keep an eye on the situation. Still I feel like a wimp."

Her heart broke for him as she rose and sat on the arm of his chair, her palm sliding across his shoulders. "Devon, you're far from a wimp. You fight fires. You save lives while endangering your own." As soon as the words slipped from her mouth, she wanted to swallow them back. "You're brave. The best part is you're caring and that's why you avoided a confrontation. Something good will happen. I sense it. And Renee will make sure everything is all right. It makes sense."

"I hope." He reached over and pulled her onto his lap. "You are a shining star for me, Ash. You took hold of adversity and plowed your way past it. You could have crumbled or turned into a ball of flesh." His eyes sought hers. "You didn't. You lived finding joy in Joey and family. Now I find joy in the same. You, Joey and Kaylee. You make me remember darkness only lasts a while and daylight comes again."

His lips met hers, washing away all doubts and worries. Yet he had the weight of the world on his shoulders. She clung to him, praying for the answers to find their way into his life and longing for a day when she could commit to him with all fear gone. It all hung on her willingness to say the word. Today the word lay on the tip of her tongue.

He shifted his legs, and she rose, sensing he planned to stand. He did, his arms drawing her close. "Let's not waste the day worrying. I say we do something fun or constructive."

She chuckled at his options. "Summer's not here much longer so let's do something outside."

He stepped back, his hands still resting on her shoulders. "Anything with you is fun."

A sound caused her to draw back and as

she did, the doorbell rang. When she opened the door, her cousin, Paula, stepped in. "I stopped by to say goodbye for now. I'm heading back to Roscommon and getting the house cleaned out so I can put it on the market."

"I'm glad you said for now. You know we'd like you back in our lives. It's been too long, and now that your mom and dad are gone nothing keeps you in Roscommon."

Paula chuckled. "Sadly, nothing kept me there before, either." She gave a feeble shrug. "You and Neely have been great, and as you heard, I said goodbye for now. Your dad invited me to stay with him if I move to Ferndale until I get settled somewhere. He said he'd love the company."

Ashley's heart skipped. "I'm thrilled. This is what we'd hoped for." She opened her arms to her cousin, and Paula slipped into them. When she stepped back, Ashley noticed tears in her cousin's eyes. "Don't make me cry, too."

"I'm a bit emotional. No one has been so kind since I can remember." She turned toward Devon and extended her hand. "So good to meet you, and I'm pretty sure you'll still be around when I get back."

Devon chuckled. "I hope you're right."

"She is." Ashley couldn't stop from speaking the truth. She'd be lost without him.

She walked Paula to the door and waited until she pulled away, when she turned, Devon had vanished. She closed the door and found him in the kitchen leaning against the counter, his cell phone pressed against his ear.

Instead of eavesdropping, she backed away and returned to the living room, curious about the call.

A few moments later, Devon returned and leaned his shoulder against the archway. "That was Kaylee. Of all things, she is crying. She wants to come home. That put me on the spot."

"What did you say?" Her pulse skittered up her arm.

"I told her to talk with her mother and reminded her I have to work tomorrow."

Ashley dragged in air. "Now you're the one in the middle."

"I suppose, but I know Kaylee's fine. Renee

went home as she promised, and since Gina is avoiding me, Kaylee has the best chance at being honest with Gina about where she wants to live." He rubbed his palm across his jaw. "She's only four. It's too much for her."

"But she's bright and has a keen sense of things. Maybe this is the Lord's answer." Maybe not, but nothing else made any sense.

Devon looked at Ashley, a faint grin finding its way to her face. "That's my hope." He rose and reached for her hand. "Let's wake up that boy of yours—I assume he's napping—and get out of here. Remember, we're planning to have fun."

"Joey'll love it."

He drew her into his arms, his kiss deep and warm. "I care so much for you both. I hope you know that."

"I do." She kissed him back before heading for the stairs, grateful for Devon's resolve and grateful her own resolve grew stronger by the minute.

Devon lowered the weights onto the stand and wiped perspiration from his face. Sometimes he'd prefer taking a break, but this was his job, and keeping fit was imperative. He scanned the exercise room and then the clock. He'd been at it a half hour. Today that was enough. He'd heard nothing more from Kaylee, and though he wondered, he assumed no call meant she'd agreed to stay with her mother until his next day off. Again as he headed for the door, his cell phone sounded. He stepped into the hallway and checked the ID.

His chest constricted. Gina. He hit the answer button, but before he could speak, she began.

"Kaylee's crying again and won't stop." Her voice rang with panic. "I can't take this."

A vise tightened his chest. "Why is she upset?"

"She told me she lived with you now, and I told her... How did that happen, Devon? What did you do?"

His grip tightened on the phone, and he swallowed. "What I thought was right. That's what I did. You've been sick a long time, and Renee is the one raising our daughter. Kaylee asked to live with me, and how could I say no? Tell me." Amid her silence, he detected a sniffle, and though he didn't want to hurt her, he had no choice.

"She wants to live with you, I know…but I wanted to spend time with her, Devon." Her murmur faded. "I can't force her to stay, but I want visitation. I demand it."

"Gina, I'd never deny you that." He closed his eyes praying he'd never have to. "We've always had joint custody. I'll take physical custody and you'll still have visitation rights, and when you're better, we can talk about this again, but for now living with me is best for Kaylee."

More silence. "Will I get better?"

He caught another sob.

"Come and get her, Devon. She wants to go home."

Home. His emotions bounced from sorrow for Gina and joy for himself. "I'm working today. Can she wait until—"

"I promised her she could go now. Come and get her."

Ashley rose in his thoughts. "I'll call my neighbor. She'll be there soon. If not, I'll get back to you."

"Goodbye, Devon."

She hung up and he stood in place, startled by her abrupt goodbye. The words held a strange tone, as if... He shook his head. Gina would accept the change eventually and perhaps make a greater effort to spend time with Kaylee when she was there. That was his hope.

His fingers trembled as he hit Ashley's phone number, and when she heard the news, her joy was as strong as his. Having Kaylee with him had been his dream, a complicated one until Ashley came along.

As he walked toward his office, the fire alarm broke through the air, followed by the intercom. His joy vanished as he ran for his bunker gear.

Ashley stood outside the car as Kaylee darted down the steps. She longed to embrace the child, but the frail woman watching from the doorway certainly was Gina, and she didn't want to rub salt in the wound of their parting. She grasped the rear door and opened it, encouraging Kaylee inside, and with a last look she pulled away, trying to imagine a mother's anguish when her daughter chose her father's house as home.

"Are you okay?" She glanced in the rear-view mirror before she pulled away.

Kaylee's eyes shifted from her mother lingering at the doorway to her craning over the seat. "I wanted to go home, and my mom didn't want me to, but now she said I can live with Daddy."

"I heard. I'm glad, Kaylee."

"I like being at your house, too." Her voice skipped over the seat. "I can play and be happy."

"I like to play, Kaylee." Joey reached toward her from his car seat and touched her arm.

"You're like a little brother, Joey."

"I'm not little."

Ashley had heard the discussion before, and her mind wandered, pleased that the issue had been resolved and with Gina making the custody decision. Devon would have physical custody and Gina, visitation. Their prayers were answered.

As she approached Nine Mile, a fire siren sounded and traffic skidded to a stop. The engine tore across Woodward Avenue. Her heart rose to her throat, and Joey let out an excited yell as the truck flew past. When traffic cleared, she glanced down Nine Mile. The fire engine headed west, and it was likely a two-alarm fire. Smoke rose in the distance, and her pulse skipped.

"Was my daddy in the fire truck?"

"That was a truck from Station 2, Kaylee. Your daddy's at headquarters." Which means he was closer to the fire. She swallowed her worry, and a plan flew into her mind. "Would you like to go and visit?"

"Yes, let's go see Daddy at the fire."

"We can't distract him, sweetie. I thought you might like to go and visit Grandpa for a while."

"Grandpa. Let's go." Joey's voice overpowered Kaylee's.

Breathing a relieved sigh, Ashley turned toward her father's home, anxious to let the kids play there while she went to check on the fire. It looked like a bad one.

Grateful for her dad's willingness, she left the kids, hugged her dad and tore back to

Nine Mile where traffic had already backed up. She could see flames in the distance, and her concern grew. She knew Devon had fought hundreds of fires, but she didn't know him then, didn't love him then.

Love. The word sizzled in her mind. She'd avoided letting it sneak out and had used every other descriptive form of caring, but today love clung to her thoughts. She adored Devon. Cherished him. Longed for him in her life...forever.

Unable to negotiate the roadblock and traffic, she turned and headed back. She knew better than to be a gawker like those people who chased tragic situations. She grimaced at her decision to go there, but seeing the tragedy made her know where her heart had led her.

Her father's eyes widened when she came through the door. "You're back already?"

She shrugged, not wanting the children to know what she'd done. "I ran into traffic and a roadblock. Wisdom finally opened my eyes."

He nodded. "Good choice. You don't need to see that and worry."

"I know, Daddy." She kissed his cheek and settled into a chair. "Where are the kids?"

"Neely dropped by and heard the good news from Kaylee, so she took them out for ice cream. Hope you don't mind."

"No, it's better. They did see the fire truck and asked about Devon." She lowered her head a minute. "Dad, I'm crazy about him, and I've worried about his dangerous job, but I'm ready to give up the battle and open my heart and my arms."

A huge grin filled her father's face. "I knew you couldn't resist a good man like that for long. You've made a wonderful decision. I know he loves you."

"I think he does." She drew in a lengthy breath. "I hope Neely isn't gone, too—" Her cell phone played its tune, and she glanced at the number. Her stomach tightened into a knot. The caller ID read Clint Donatelli. The only reason he would call was…

Tears brimmed in her eyes as she pressed the button. "Clint, what happened?"

"Ashley, Devon asked me to call you. He fell through the flooring. His leg was injured."

"His leg. Is it—"

"They don't think it's serious, but they took him to Beaumont Hospital."

"In Royal Oak?"

"That's the one. He wanted you to know. He told me to tell you not to worry. He doesn't think it's serious, but—"

"Thanks so much for letting me know. I'll head over there." She hung up as fear gripped her. The horrible call she'd anticipated had happened. If this was the beginning of what she had to face for the rest of her life, she'd... She would nothing. Her thoughts fell away to dust. It was too late. She loved him and fear couldn't make the love go away. When she turned to her dad, she didn't have to explain.

"Get over there, my girl, and don't worry about the kids. I'll keep them entertained."

"Thanks, Daddy. They don't think it's serious, but..." She pressed her lips together to keep from crying.

"Go."

Her love for her father swept over her. "Yes, sir."

He chuckled as she raced out the door.

Ashley tore into emergency and headed for the admissions station. "Devon Murphy was just brought in. He's a firefight—"

"Are you a relative?"

Fearing the woman would stop her, she longed to lie and say his wife, but she wouldn't. "I'm his…"

"Girlfriend?" The woman eyed her.

"Yes, and he had one of the firefighters call."

A faint grin flickered on the woman's face. "He's in triage six."

Ashley hit the large button and the door slid open. She checked the numbers, hurried to the curtain and slipped it open.

Devon's eyes shifted. "Ash."

Though relief filled his face, she noted the concern in his eyes. She already knew what he feared. "I thank God you're okay." She shifted beside him, and lowered her lips to his cheek. "What's the diagnosis?"

"A sprain. My leg went through the flooring and it twisted when I went down." His mouth curved to a grin. "Looks like I'll need to borrow your crutches."

"You're too tall, but I'll be very happy to see you get a brand-new pair. How's it feel?"

"Swollen and painful, but nothing horrible. They gave me something for pain." He reached up and slipped his fingers through hers. "I wondered if you'd come."

Shame burrowed into her chest, and she lowered her head. "Devon." She forced her chin upward, her eyes capturing his. "Nothing could have kept me away. Not anymore." The truth gave her instant relief.

"But I know how much you've worried about this kind of thing—the telephone call you never wanted to receive—and I'd insisted I've never been injured and suggested that I never would."

"We can get hurt driving a car or walking a dog. Didn't you remind me of that?"

He nodded. "But I know how the fear of something happening has affected you."

She pressed her finger against his lips. "Not anymore. I promise."

"No?" His eyes prodded hers. "What made you change your mind?"

"You."

"Me?"

"I can't live without you, Devon. I finally realized you're everything I'd ever wanted, and I think this was in the plan forever." Her confidence grew with each word. "Things happen when we least expect them. Not just a tree falling on top of a person, but meeting a soul mate."

"I'm hoping that's me." He grinned, his expression sparking with life and love.

"You know it is." She chuckled. "I'd get on one knee and propose, but you'd probably only see the top of my head, lying on this gurney, and I want to look you in the eyes when I do."

"I'm looking?" He moved her hand and pressed it against his heart.

"Devon Murphy, will you marry me?" She stopped his words with the flex of her left hand. "But promise you'll never tell anyone I proposed."

His grin blossomed to a smile. "Come on. Don't ruin the fun. I've never had a woman propose to me before." He tilted his head forward and kissed her hand.

She sent him a playful frown. "And I hope you never do again."

He chuckled. "Before you withdraw those tantalizing words, I'll accept your proposal, and I won't tell a soul."

She leaned down, her lips molding into his as if they'd kiss for a lifetime. When she caught her breath, her joy grew. "I can't wait until we tell the kids."

"We'll tell them together. And I think it's time for you to meet my parents. They've heard all about you."

"They have?"

"They love you already."

She brushed his cheek with her palm, tears in her eyes, a grin on her lips.

"I should be out of here today. They already wrapped my leg in an elastic wrap and told me to put cold compresses on the sprain for twenty minutes every two hours, elevate my leg, use crutches and rest."

"Rest." She gave him a wink. "That means you'll be off work."

He grinned. "For a while, and I'll need a pretty caregiver to pamper me."

"And I know the perfect person to do just that."

He drew her closer and kissed her again, the longest, deepest kiss she'd ever experienced.

Devon sat in Ashley's recliner, his leg propped on the footrest with a pillow beneath and his crutches balanced against the lamp table. He'd knocked them down more than once trying to snatch them, but Ashley or one of the kids always came to his rescue. Though his leg ached off and on throughout the day, he still smiled at the memory of Ashley proposing, a moment when his dream had come true.

The kids had responded as he'd expected, with a robust response of yelling and hand clapping. The scene lifted his spirits and filled him with joy, especially to see Kaylee glowing with happiness. She'd lived through many difficulties and yet she'd survived and flourished. He had to thank Renee, and even Gina did the best she could. He couldn't fault her for her illness and despite it, she'd given him the gift of custody, an event he never thought could happen without a fight.

And his parents were jubilant when he called them. They loved the idea of adding a grandson to the family. Their joy melded with his happiness, and he knew they planned to visit on Saturday.

Kaylee sauntered into the room and stood near him, her face filled with anxiety. Her look surprised him, and a hitch of concern caught in his chest. How had her joyful response to their announcement turned to worry?

"What's wrong, sweetie?" He opened his arms, and she came to his side, steering clear of his injured leg.

She shrugged, her head turning to glance toward the kitchen where Ashley was preparing dinner. When she turned back, her expression had changed. "I don't know what to call—" She tilted her head toward the kitchen "—Ashley. Can I call her Mommy when you get married?"

Her question threw him off guard and he hesitated, not knowing how to answer.

"You can, but you have a mommy already, sweetie."

"I know." Her eyes filled with question. "Can't I have two?"

Her question left a lump in his throat. "You can, but do you think your other mommy might have hurt feelings if you call Ashley the same thing?"

Her eyes shifted to the ceiling as if in thought, and then she looked at him. "I'll call her Ashley when I'm with Mommy." She drew closer and stood beside the chair, resting her head on his shoulder. "But Ashley is like a real mommy, too, who hugs me, and reads to me, and tells me when I do something bad."

"Did you do something bad?" He arched a brow, wanting to laugh at her expression. Behind her, Ashley stood in the doorway, her lips pressed together to control her emotions.

"She would if I did something bad cuz she tells me when I'm good."

"That's the kind of mommy to have, isn't it?"

She nodded.

"We haven't set a date yet, sweetheart, and when we're married, you can call Ashley whatever makes you happy. I know Ashley will love being your other mom."

Ashley brushed a tear from her eye and backed away.

A lump caught in his chest. Kaylee had experienced far more than any four-year-old should, and knowing one day she would have the joy of a healthy mom who truly loved her. He could see that in Ashley's face each time she looked at his daughter.

Kaylee leaned over and kissed his cheek. "Did I hurt your leg?"

"Not one bit. You made it feel better."

"Can we go out and buy Ashley a wedding ring?"

He chuckled. "When I can get around better, I'll let you look at some with me, okay?"

"Yay!" She jumped from the chair arm and ran into the kitchen, her announcement resonating through the house.

Joey darted into the room. "Mommy said it's dinnertime. You should wash your hands."

"Was that message for me or you?"

His nose crinkled and he ran away giggling as he headed for the bathroom.

Devon managed to grab his crutches before

they slipped from his grasp, and after easing down the footrest, he used his good leg to stand and propped the crutches beneath his arms. Now he could sympathize with Ashley's weeks on the wooden props. The experience wasn't one he wanted to deal with again, but he had thanked the Lord over and over that he had escaped any more damage than a sprain.

When they were seated around the table, they bowed their heads for the blessing, and when he said amen, Kaylee broke in with an added petition.

"Let's say thank you to Jesus for our new family." She lifted her head as a frown grew on her face. "Our new family one day... when you get married." The knitted brows smoothed with her smile. "Cuz being a family is the best thing. It's like the best puzzle in the world."

His eyes widened as he tried to make sense. "How is family like a puzzle?"

She grinned. "It's lots of pieces that have to be put together, fixing the mistakes and then putting in the last piece and seeing a beautiful picture. We'll be the picture."

Tears dripped from Ashley's eyes, and she hurried to Kaylee's side and drew her into a hug. "That was the loveliest thing I've heard in years…and even more amazing because it came from a four-year-old."

"But I'll be five soon, and then I'll be older than Joey."

Devon couldn't contain himself. His laughter burst into the open, realizing they'd come full circle. "Kaylee."

She looked at him, her expression questioning. "Did I do something bad?"

"Not at all. I love you more than words can tell." He opened his arms and drew her in. "In fact, I need to hug everyone so all the puzzle pieces are together."

Joey bounded to him, and Ashley squeezed into the circle between the children. Her gaze drifted to the children, and then caught his eyes. "Let the puzzle say amen."

Their voices weaved together with a bold amen, and the moment tucked into Devon's heart, and he knew it would never leave. His personal amen lifted heavenward.

* * * * *

Dear Reader,

I hope you've enjoyed the second novel in the Sisters series. You met Neely in *Her Valentine Hero,* and now you know her sister, Ashley, even better. Ashley's and Devon's struggles, though different, were similar. Each struggle dealt with a marriage that ended too soon. In our world today young widows raise their children without a father, and our mental health system does not meet the needs of many adults and children struggling with forms of mental illness. Such illnesses affect families.

Ashley and Devon were also heroes, their focus on protecting their children and their hearts. Sometimes life seems difficult, but we Christians can cling to our belief in Jesus. If we have faith and trust in God's love and mercy, we are able to release life's burdens and lay them at Jesus' feet. When Ashley and Devon clung to the Lord, they found the answers they needed. Let us follow their example and give our burdens and praise to the Lord.

Wishing you blessings and an invitation to drop by my website at www.gailgaymermartin.com and say hello.

Gail Gaymer Martin

Questions for Discussion

1. Does someone in your life raise their child/children as a single parent? Are their problems similar or different from Ashley's and in what way?

2. Ashley worked from her home. This allowed her to be with Joey and still earn a living. Do you know anyone who works from their home? What jobs are available for working out of the home? Can the person earn a living?

3. What are some ways employers could help single parents?

4. Do you know a firefighter personally? How does his/her career affect the individual's life? What are the pros and cons of a career like this?

5. Ashley lost her husband in Afghanistan and now fears falling in love with a firefighter. Is her fear realistic? Why? If not, why not?

6. What experience in your past causes you to avoid relationships or other aspects of your life? Or have you been able to overcome the fear, and if so, how?

7. Ashley and Devon referred to the scripture from Proverb 3:5, *Trust in the Lord with all your heart and lean not on your own understanding.* What does this verse mean to you?

8. Can you understand or relate to the mother-daughter struggle that Ashley, Neely and Paula experienced? Have situations in your life resulted in strained relationships with you and a parent?

9. The children played a big role in this novel. How did they affect your enjoyment of the story?

10. Devon worried about putting Kaylee in the middle of a custody battle even though she wanted to live with her father. Do you think Devon's concern was right and why?

11. What qualities did you admire about Ashley and Devon as parents?

12. We've heard Jesus say in Matthew 12:16 *Out of the mouth of infants...* Kaylee's comparison of a puzzle to the new family was unique and does express that children's view of life is bold and different from adults'. Their praise is from the heart, and so was her comparison. How did that comparison relate to your own family?

REQUEST YOUR FREE BOOKS!

2 FREE RIVETING INSPIRATIONAL NOVELS IN TRUE LARGE PRINT PLUS 2 FREE MYSTERY GIFTS

YES! Please send me 2 FREE Love Inspired® Suspense True Large Print novels and my 2 FREE mystery gifts (gifts are worth about $10). After receiving them, if I don't wish to receive any more books, I can return the shipping statement marked "cancel." If I don't cancel, I will receive 3 brand-new true large print novels every month and be billed just $7.99 per book in the U.S. or $9.99 per book in Canada. That's a savings of at least 20% off the cover price. It's quite a bargain! Shipping and handling is just 50¢ per book in the U.S. and 75¢ per book in Canada.* I understand that accepting the 2 free books and gifts places me under no obligation to buy anything. I can always return the shipment and cancel at any time. Even if I never buy another book, the two free books and gifts are mine to keep forever.

124/324 IDN F5GD

Name _____ (PLEASE PRINT)

Address _____ Apt. # _____

City _____ State/Prov. _____ Zip/Postal Code _____

Signature (if under 18, a parent or guardian must sign)

Mail to the Harlequin® Reader Service:
IN U.S.A.: P.O. Box 1867, Buffalo, NY 14240-1867
IN CANADA: P.O. Box 609, Fort Erie, Ontario L2A 5X3

* Terms and prices subject to change without notice. Prices do not include applicable taxes. Sales tax applicable in N.Y. Canadian residents will be charged applicable taxes. Offer not valid in Quebec. This offer is limited to one order per household. Not valid for current subscribers to Love Inspired Suspense True Large Print books. All orders subject to credit approval. Credit or debit balances in a customer's account(s) may be offset by any other outstanding balance owed by or to the customer. Please allow 4 to 6 weeks for delivery. Offer available while quantities last.

Your Privacy—The Harlequin® Reader Service is committed to protecting your privacy. Our Privacy Policy is available online at www.ReaderService.com or upon request from the Harlequin Reader Service.

We make a portion of our mailing list available to reputable third parties that offer products we believe may interest you. If you prefer that we not exchange your name with third parties, or if you wish to clarify or modify your communication preferences, please visit us at www.ReaderService.com/consumerschoice or write to us at Harlequin Reader Service Preference Service, P.O. Box 9062, Buffalo, NY 14269. Include your complete name and address.

LISTLP13TRR

REQUEST YOUR FREE BOOKS!

2 FREE INSPIRATIONAL NOVELS IN TRUE LARGE PRINT

PLUS 2 FREE MYSTERY GIFTS

Love Inspired®

TRUE LARGE PRINT

YES! Please send me 2 FREE Love Inspired® True Large Print novels and my 2 FREE mystery gifts (gifts are worth about $10). After receiving them, if I don't wish to receive any more books, I can return the shipping statement marked "cancel." If I don't cancel, I will receive 3 brand-new true large print novels every month and be billed just $7.99 per book in the U.S. or $9.99 per book in Canada. That's a savings of at least 20% off the cover price. It's quite a bargain! Shipping and handling is just 50¢ per book in the U.S. and 75¢ per book in Canada.* I understand that accepting the 2 free books and gifts places me under no obligation to buy anything. I can always return the shipment and cancel at any time. Even if I never buy another book, the two free books and gifts are mine to keep forever.

117/317 IDN F5FZ

Name	(PLEASE PRINT)

Address	Apt. #

City	State/Prov.	Zip/Postal Code

Signature (if under 18, a parent or guardian must sign)

Mail to the **Harlequin® Reader Service:**
IN U.S.A.: P.O. Box 1867, Buffalo, NY 14240-1867
IN CANADA: P.O. Box 609, Fort Erie, Ontario L2A 5X3

* Terms and prices subject to change without notice. Prices do not include applicable taxes. Sales tax applicable in N.Y. Canadian residents will be charged applicable taxes. Offer not valid in Quebec. This offer is limited to one order per household. Not valid for current subscribers to Love Inspired True Large Print books. All orders subject to credit approval. Credit or debit balances in a customer's account(s) may be offset by any other outstanding balance owed by or to the customer. Please allow 4 to 6 weeks for delivery. Offer available while quantities last.

Your Privacy—The Harlequin® Reader Service is committed to protecting your privacy. Our Privacy Policy is available online at www.ReaderService.com or upon request from the Harlequin Reader Service.

We make a portion of our mailing list available to reputable third parties that offer products we believe may interest you. If you prefer that we not exchange your name with third parties, or if you wish to clarify or modify your communication preferences, please visit us at www.ReaderService.com/consumerschoice or write to us at Harlequin Reader Service Preference Service, P.O. Box 9062, Buffalo, NY 14269. Include your complete name and address.

Reader Service.com

Manage your account online!
- Review your order history
- Manage your payments
- Update your address

> ### *We've designed the Harlequin® Reader Service website just for you.*

Enjoy all the features!
- Reader excerpts from any series
- Respond to mailings and special monthly offers
- Discover new series available to you
- Browse the Bonus Bucks catalogue
- Share your feedback

Visit us at:

ReaderService.com

RS13TR